PROJECT AMI

Emiel Sleegers

NOTEBOOK|PUBLISHING

First published in the UK in 2015 by Notebook Publishing,
145–157 St John Street, London, EC1V 4PW.

www.notebookpublishing.co

ISBN: 9780993589805
Copyright © Emiel Sleegers 2016.

A CIP catalogue record for this book is available
from the British Library.

Typeset by Notebook Publishing.
Printed and bound in Great Britain.

DEDICATION

For my parents:

Your support is all the inspiration I need.

PROLOGUE

THE BEGINNING

It has been three years since the attack.

It all happened on November 24, 2042. And it was on that day the Hacker group, who called themselves Zero, launched an attack on a global scale. By that time, it was common to have a 'helper bot' to assist in and around the house, to make life easier. But Zero had come along and launched a virus that successfully turned every helper bot into a killer.

At first, we did not think much of it: there were some bots affected by the virus, and they started to attack humans. But we managed to control it. And, really, there was damage-limited and procedures in place to prevent any significant spread of the problem—wasn't there?

But after a while longer, more and more bots started to become affected, and slowly they started to overrun us. They started to develop a mind of their own. They learned to use weapons, how to manipulate humans, how to take control—and all of this spanning the globe.

They say that even the hacker group did not expect things to become so big, to get so out of hand.

The bots slowly and systematically started to kill every living thing they could find.

We began to call them KBs—Killer Bots.

Since then, three years have passed, and the KBs managed to wipe out around three-quarters of the entire human population. Now, the only thing left for humans to do is try to survive. Sure, we have some resistance groups scattered around the areas, but all they can do is perform small operations to give the KBs a hard time. But in the end, the KBs always win.

Most of the big cities and villages are abounded now. The KBs rule every urban area there is.

So most people have retreated to the forests and sewers. Those places are hard to reach.

But this means no electricity.

No infrastructure.

And food and water sources are scarce.

In this world, only one thing matters.

Surviving.

CHAPTER 1

A NEW FRIEND

It is late in the afternoon. You see a boy running through the forest. He looks scared and tired. You can see that he has had a hard time; his clothes are ripped. His blue jeans can barely be called jeans anymore. He is wearing a dirty t-shirt with a leather jacket that has been ripped off at the bottom. He is struggling to run, the large army backpack weighing him down.

There are three KBs running behind him, and they shoot.

The boy jumps over a log, grabs his pistol from his back, and starts to shoot whilst running forward. He fires four shots, one of which hits one of the KBs straight in the head. The KB falls over and crashes against a tree. The boy continues to shoot at the other two KBs, but he is so focused on them that he does not notice he is heading straight for a steep hill. Suddenly, he falls over and tumbles down the hill. At the bottom, he comes to a stop. He takes a few moments to analyse what happened, and then quickly he crawls behind a big tree. He peeks out behind the tree and sees the two KBs slowly heading down the hill.

They are big, and even though they have the same shape as a human, they do not have actual skin; they are more made from some kind of transparent plastic. Their wiring and electronics can be seen passing this way and that through their body—and that's a good thing because this communicates one vital point: they're plastic and so not so strong and easier to kill.

It looks like that they have lost him, and they start to search. He waits for them to pass along the bottom of the hill, and there he sees them heading in different directions; one heads in his direction. The boy takes a knife that is strapped to his boot. He makes himself small and stays behind the tree, ready to jump out. He listens intently as the KB moves closer and closer still, and the boy positions himself ready for the attack.

The KB walks past him and, when he is about to turn around, the boy jumps up from behind the tree and stabs his knife into the chest of the KB. The robot makes a slight noise—almost like a beeping noise, the volume slowly decreasing.

The boy quickly grabs his gun again and checks if the other KB has heard him, but he looks to be too far away to have heard anything. He walks over to the KB and, at that moment, the KB turns around and the boy shoots two bullets, straight into his chest. *A perfect aim.*

The boy walks back to the tree, picks up his backpack and, with an angry but relieved stance, starts to walk along the hillside.

The boy walks and walks. He walks further still, but then he stumbles upon a concrete structure, imbedded into the ground; it looks like a square block, sticking up out of the hill. But that is not the strangest part: there is a metal door in the centre.

The boy inspects the door and sees a chain lock across it. He hesitates and wonders whether he should break in to see what's inside, but then he reminds himself that he is running low on supplies and there could be food and water in there. He looks at the lock and sees that it is a number lock requiring a four-digit code. He tries out a few obvious codes, trying his luck; 0000 and 1234. None of them work.

'Screw this,' he mutters. 'I don't have time for this.' He takes out his pistol. He aims it at the lock, looks away, and shoots the lock off. The lock breaks away with ease, and the boy tries to open the door, but still the door appears to be locked. With the back of his gun, he hits the knob a few times and then starts to kick against the door. After a few tries, the door breaks open, and the boy soon finds himself in a big hall.

Everything looks very modern; the floor is shiny and wooden, and the walls are made of white panels. He walks through the hall to find a big double door at the end. He opens the door and he enters into what looks like a living room.

Everything looks more modern than the boy is used to: there is a large TV hanging against the wall;

there are leather couches and chairs; and there is a bar positioned in the back. Light shines through the big windows on the side of the living room.

He walks over at the bar and there he sees a bottle of scotch. He takes the bottle and puts it in his backpack. He looks to his left and there he sees another metal door. Walking through, he finds himself in a dark room with only a little light shining in from the living room. There are a few electric wires running into the room, and he decides to follow them. The wires lead to an old-fashioned fuel generator. He checks to see whether there is any fuel left in it. He flips a switch and presses a green button, and the generator makes a loud grumbling noise. Shortly after, the lights flicker on.

The room is lit up by bright white lights, and the boy takes a moment to adjust his eyes. Soon after, he sees he is standing in the middle of a high-tech lab. He looks around him and sees computers, microscopes and loose electronics. He looks to his right and there he sees what looks like a few KBs. With fear racing through his chest, he aims his gun at them but does not shoot. He waits, expecting them to move, but nothing happens. He takes a closer look and sees that they look different to the default KBs; they look more modern somehow. He moves closer still and sees that some of the bots are incomplete. Most are missing parts of their body, like hands and legs, and some have parts of their body covered in skin—like human skin.

The boy comes closer to one of the bots with skin on her arms and head. Very carefully, he reaches out and touches the skin. It feels like human skin, but is very cold with a hard foundation. The rest of the body is covered in a sort of white plastic that outlines the shape of the body.

The boy backs away and starts to look in some of the drawers to see if he can find anything useful, but there is nothing to be found and so he walks out of the room and in to the hall.

'What the hell is this place?' he says to himself.

He walks through the door at the end of the hallway, and there he ends up in a hall with big glass windows. At the end of the hall, he sees a large window almost covering the entire wall, and beyond there seems to be a normal lounge. He looks at the room, and there he sees movement: a girl walking around.

He stares and takes a few steps back. He grabs his gun and then slowly moves forward. When he is just a few feet away, he realises: she is not a real person. She looks like one of the bots he saw in the other room.

Her hands and legs are made of skin. Her head also appears to look like it has skin, but when he looks closer he can see that the back of her head is made from metal. The rest of her body is a white plastic that is slightly opaque. The wires and mechanics behind the white plastic seem to show a hearth behind her chest. He takes a few steps closer, and that is when the girl notices him.

Her voice is startled and frightened. '*Who are you?*' she asks.

The boy takes a few more steps and looks at her. Her movements are very smooth as she walks, and the way she moves her arms is nothing like a KB.

'*What are you doing here?*' asks the bot.

The boy moves a bit closer until he is almost in

front of the glass. The girl stares back and looks even more frightened.

'Are you one of them?' the boy asks.

'One of *who*?'

'One of the other bots that have been wiping us out for the past three years!' the boy answers, frustration tangible in his voice.

'I don't know what you're talking about! Who are you?'

The boy replies, 'My name is Ryan. Who are you?'

'My name is Ami,' she replies. 'You aren't allowed to come here. Are you going to hurt me?'

The boy, surprised, tells her, 'I'm not going to hurt you if you don't hurt me.'

She starts to calm down and moves closer. She looks at Ryan.

'What are you doing here, Ami?'

'What do you mean?' she asks. 'I live here.'

'Are you a bot?'

'I am an AI, if that's what you mean,' Ami responds.

'How long have you been here?'

'I have been here all my life. Do you know where my dad is?'

'Your dad?'

'He's been gone for a really long time now.' A look of sadness passes over her face. 'I am afraid that something happened to him.'

'Can you tell me who your dad is?' Ryan asks, concern furrowing his brow.

'Well, I always call him Dad but his real name is James. He's the one who created me. He always calls me his special girl.' She smiles. 'He almost always wears a black t-shirt and blue jeans.'

'You're very calm,' Ryan observes.

'What do you mean? Why would I not be calm? You don't seem dangerous to me!'

'Do you have any idea what the outside world is like?' He almost laughs.

'Well, my dad did show me some pictures once. He showed me pictures of beautiful landscapes and big cities. He once showed me a video about how people live in the city.'

Ryan nods.

'Why are you asking all these questions? Did

something happen? Is my dad okay?'

'Well, I don't know your dad, so I don't know if he's okay,' Ryan responds, 'but what I do know is the outside world is not how it was on your pictures. Three years ago a virus turned any helper bot bad. They've killed a lot of people and have taken over a big part of the world.'

Amy thinks on this, and shakes her head sadly.

'You are a bot but somehow you look and feel different. It's like you're a newer model,' Ryan comments.

Ami looks scared. 'What's a virus? And how do I know if my dad is okay? The last time I saw him he was very worried. He told me to stay here and that he would be back soon. And still, I am waiting…'

Ryan tells her that he does not know. He steps back and walks into a different room.

'Wait! Where are you going? 'Ami asks urgently.

'I'm just going to look around. I'll be back soon,' he replies.

He walks into another room and finds an office, and there he walks over to a big wooden desk at the back of the room. Stacks of paper, detailing mathematics and blueprints, are mounted on the desk. He picks up one of the blueprints; it details a bot that looks a lot like the girl in the other room. At the top he sees a title: Project Ami 2043.

'Hmm… Year 1 after the attack,' he muses. 'She must be a newer model and somehow the virus did not reach her.'

Ryan steps behind the desk and sits down in the big office chair. He opens one of the drawers and there he finds more drawings. Most of the drawings depict parts of the room the girl is in, but there is also a drawing of a man. The sketch is in black and white. The man has a clean-shaved face and long hair. Ryan takes the drawing and walks back into the hallway. He walks to Ami and holds the drawing against the glass. With a kind voice he asks, 'Is this your dad?'

'Yes, that's him!' She smiles. 'I drew that a long time ago. My dad taught me how to draw, and I made that drawing for his birthday.'

Ryan smiles.

'Do you have a dad?' she asks.

The boy looks down and can feel the sadness creep across his face. He tells Ami that he lost his family in the first year of the attack.

'I'm so sorry,' she replies.

'It's okay. It was a long time ago.' He looks around again and then shrugs his shoulders. 'Well, it's getting late. I think it's time for me to go.'

'Wait! Are you going to leave me? I don't want to be alone anymore! Please, let me come with you! I promise I will do whatever you say!'

'I'm not sure about that. How do I know I can trust you?' Ryan asks. 'You are a bot after all.'

'No, wait, please! I swear I'll behave and I will follow your lead.' Ami's face expresses sadness, so strong it draws the boy's attention.

How can a bot express emotions like that? he wonders. 'Okay, you can come with me, but one false move and I will put you down.'

'Thank you so much! I promise I'll behave,' she says with excitement.

Ryan walks to the door next to the glass window. He tries to open the door but it looks like there is no handle. All he can see is a square box next to the door. He asks Ami, 'Do you know how I can open the door?'

'My dad always laid his hand on that little box and then the door would open,' she responds.

Ryan tries to put his hand on the scanner, but a 'not recognised' error flashes up.

He tells Ami that he has a better idea, and tells her to stand back. He then takes out his gun and shoots the scanner. The scanner shatters in million pieces, but the door opens.

Ami walk to the door and opens it further. She walks through it and stands in front of Ryan. He hesitates, still unsure, but he is prepared to shoot if needed. She asks where he wants to go, and he tells her they first will go outside, then they will walk north until the sun goes down, and after that they will set up camp and stay put for the night.

Ryan turns around and starts to walk towards the exit of the building. Ami walks behind him, looking around, a big smile on her face.

They stand in front of the door that leads outside. Ryan stops Ami and tells her that the world outside is dangerous. He tells her she needs to follow his every lead. Ami nods and tells Ryan she will not disappoint him. With a smile, he then opens the door and together they step outside.

'Wow! This looks amazing! Look at all the colours!' Ami exclaims with wonder.

Ryan laughs. 'Follow me.'

They start to walk past the hillside. The sun hangs low in the sky, and there is a beautiful sun shining through the trees. The birds sing.

Ami is truly amazed. She looks around, awe emblazoned across her face. Ryan smiles and tells her to stay close.

After walking through the forest for a while, Ryan notices that the sun is getting lower and lower. He tells Ami they need to set up camp before it gets too dark. They start to walk a bit deeper into the forest, and Ryan finds a good place with cover. He tells Ami he will look for some dry wood to make a fire. A few minutes later, he returns. Ami sits in the grass, touching everything, happiness radiating from her. Ryan lays the dry wood. He takes his backpack and removes some old newspapers from it and stuffs them between the wood. He then takes out a lighter and lights the paper.

Ami gets closer and looks at the fire. 'Look at the colours!' she says.

Ryan looks in his backpack for some food, and then all of a sudden hears 'Ow!'

He quickly looks up and sees that Ami is holding her hand, a pained expression on her face. 'I touched the fire but it was really hot!'

'You can feel heat?' he asks in surprise.

'Yes, of course. I can feel the same things you can. Why wouldn't I be able to?'

'Ami, can I ask you something?'

'Of course.'

'Why where you locked up in that room?'

'Well, when I was made, my dad showed special interest in me. He put me in that room and every day he came and we talked for hours. He would tell me a lot of different stories, sometime happy ones and sometimes scary ones. There were always cameras around, recording my emotions. My dad tells me it is not normal for a bot to have feelings. I think that's why he always called me his special girl. He thought I was unique.'

Ryan leans closer. 'Wait… You're saying you can feel emotions?'

'Of course.' Confusion creases her forehead, as if providing Ryan with proof. 'Is it really so strange for a bot to have emotions?'

'I think you are probably the only bot in the world to *feel* anything,' he responds. 'You must be truly special.'

Ami smiles. 'So where will we be going tomorrow?'

'I'll tell you that in the morning. For now, today was a long day, and all I want to do now is get some sleep.'

'Okay,' she replies. 'I will wait here until you wake up.'

Ryan takes his sleeping bag from his backpack, rolls it out, and crawls into it. He looks at Ami one last time and sees her staring into the fire.

'Today has been a good day,' she says into the flames.

He smiles before making himself comfortable and slowly falling to sleep.

CHAPTER 2

BARN FIND

It is early in the morning. The sun is shining through the trees, and Ryan hears a sound of someone walking around him. He stands up and looks around him, but Ami is nowhere to be seen. He jumps up, grabs his gun, and starts to walk around the camp in an effort to locate her. He calls her name but, after calling a few times, he hears a voice in the distance.

'I'm here.'

He walks towards the sound of her voice, and then calls again. Once again he hears, 'I'm here.' He is getting closer. He pushes away a few bushes and ends up on a big open field. In the field he sees a barn, with Ami standing right in front of it, looking up in wonder. He walks to Ami and asks what she is doing.

Ami replies, 'I was looking around and I found this house. Isn't it just beautiful? Shall we go inside?'

'You shouldn't run off like that, Amu. This is a dangerous place! If you don't look out, you could get wounded—or worse!'

'I'm sorry,' she says quietly. 'I just did not want to wake you up. And I was curious. And kind of lonely and bored sitting there while you slept.'

'It's okay. Did you see anybody or any bots around?'

'No, but I only just got here.'

'Okay. I will have a look, but you stay behind me.'

Ryan grabs his gun and slowly starts to walk towards the barn. It's an old structure, and scratching noises come from inside—*Rats or mice maybe?* he wonders.

Ryan takes the handle of one of the doors and throws open the door. As soon as he opens the door, a flock of doves fly out of the roof, an alert sounding from their mouths and up into the morning sky.

Ami ducks and screams.

'It's okay!' Ryan reassures her urgently. 'They're just birds.'

Ami slowly stands up and takes Ryan's arm. They start to walk into the barn. Ryan asks Ami to let go so that he can make sure everything is safe. He walks back to Ami when he is satisfied, and together they look around the barn, but all they can see are some saddles, tools and hay bales. There are holes in the back wall and the roof of the barn, and bright yellow sunlight filters through the gaps from the early-morning sun.

Ami walks to the back wall and looks through one of the holes. With an excited voice she says, 'Ryan, I can see another house through this hole!'

Ryan walks to the wall and looks through the hole. A small, wooden cabin sits in the distance, a porch at the front. Clothes hang on the railings, and everything looks clean and well-maintained. He tells Ami he will have a look to see if there is something to be found there.

'Can I come with you?' she asks.

'Okay, but stay behind me and stay low until I

tell you it's safe.'

They walk out of the barn and around the back, heading in the direction of the cabin. When they are a few feet away, all of a sudden, they are shot at from one of the windows of the cabin. Ryan quickly grabs Ami and they dive behind some wooden logs. Ryan looks at Ami and asks if she is okay. But she has been hit in the arm.

After a few seconds, however, Ryan watches in disbelief as the skin on Ami's arm closes the gaping hole. In awe, he asks, 'How did you do that?'

'I have a self-healing function that can fix small injuries and errors so that I do not become incapacitated because of a small injury.'

'So basically you're immortal?' Ryan laughs, incredulous.

'Of course not,' she smiles. 'It only works for small injuries. If he had shot me a few more times it would have been a lot worse.'

'Okay, just stay down,' Ryan commands. 'I'll handle this.'

Ryan grabs his gun and peeks out above the logs. He watches as a big man rushes outside.

Ryan yells, 'We don't want any trouble!' But the only reply they get is 'Screw you!' and the man starts shooting in their direction.

Ryan takes a few deep breaths, peeks out his head out again to look where the man is, and starts to shoot at him. The man gets hit in his leg and immediately turns to Ryan and starts shooting in his direction. Ryan tells Ami to stay put, and he walks to the left side of the logs. There he prepares himself to make a sprint to another pile of logs, and then he rushes across unseen by his enemy.

Ryan glances over the logs and sees that the man does not know where he is. He aims his gun and fires one shot. The man falls down into the grass, and everything falls quiet. Ryan waits a few moments and then walks over to the man. He looks on at the ugly guy, now lay in the grass. He wears a filthy white t-shirt that is way too small for him, and his jeans are ripped.

He approaches the guy and checks he is alive, but he is not. He calls out that it is safe, and watches as Ami appears out of cover. She looks scared, but slowly walks to Ryan.

A few feet away from him she asks if the man is dead. Ryan nods solemnly. He walks over to Ami and tells her that this is their world now and, in order to survive, they need to protect themselves.

'Come, let's check out the cabin,' Ryan suggests.

He walks to the cabin and Ami follows. Ryan has his gun ready to shoot. He opens the door and checks every corner to see if it is safe. He quickly walks into the rooms, scanning them to see if there is anybody else in the cabin. He then walks back outside and tells Ami all is clear.

Ryan walks into the kitchen to look for supplies, and then routes through closets and cupboards. He finds a few cans of food and some bottles of water. In the meantime, Ami walks into another room. Ryan checks the entire kitchen and puts the food and water into his backpack.

Ami stands in front of an open closet looking at a dress. Ran enters the room and tells her she can take it if she likes. 'It would be safer for you to wear a dress so that people think you're human and not a bot,' he says. 'Less drama that way.'

Ami picks the dress out of the closet and, with a smile on her face, holds it in front of her and looks at Ryan. 'What do you think?' she asks.

'I think it will look great on you,' he replies.

Ami takes the dress from the hanger and slowly puts it on. Ryan looks at her and smiles. 'You look just like a human,' he says.

Ami smiles, and then her attention is drawn to a mirror on the other side of the room. She sees a few foam heads with wigs on them. She walks over to the wigs and picks one up. It has short black hair. She puts on the wig and looks at herself in the mirror. With an amazed look in her eyes, she starts to smile. She turns to Ryan and, with happiness in her voice, asks, 'How do I look?'

Ryan smiles and tells her she looks beautiful.

Shyness creeps across her face, and she turns back to the mirror and inspects how she looks.

Ryan tells her they have enough food and water now and suggests they stay here for the night. He tells Ami to stay in the cabin and then he walks outside. He walks to the dead man and grabs him by his arms. With effort, he drags him a few metres and then drops him between the bushes. He picks up some branches and stray brambles, and places them on top of him. He then goes back inside and tells Ami, 'Today we can have a relaxed day. I'm going hunting later and I want you to stay here. I'm sure there is enough stuff around here to keep you busy.'

'Okay,' nods Ami with a smile.

At almost midday, Ryan walks over to his backpack and takes out a can of chili that he found in one of the cabinets. He heads into the kitchen and tests whether the stove is still working; thankfully, it looks like there is still some gas in the propane tank. He takes a pan from one of the drawers and places it on the stove. He opens the can of chili and puts it in the pan. After a while, the chili is warmed through, and Ryan takes a fork and starts eating. 'It's been so long since I have eaten this,' he says with satisfaction. 'It tastes so good!'

'I wish I could taste, but that's one thing I can't do,' Amy muses.

'Well, on the other hand, you don't need to worry about getting food or drinking water. In this world, those two things are some of the most important things for people. And a source of worry,' Ryan states.

He finishes eating and tells Ami, 'I'm going to take a quick nap and then I'll go out hunting and see if I can catch something for dinner.' He lays down on an old couch but, before he closes his eyes, he looks at Ami and tells her that if she hears anything, she should wake him up immediately.

He closes his eyes and falls asleep.

Ami continues to walk around the house to see if she can find anything interesting. She walks over to a small closet against the wall and finds some books. She picks out a book and starts reading.

A few hours later, Ryan wakes up. He stands and looks around the room. He sees Ami sitting on her knees on the ground, reading a book. 'What are you reading?' he asks.

'It's a story about a girl and a boy. They both travel around the world and keep meeting each other in different countries. After a while they fall in love and then the boy travels across the world to find her.'

Ryan laughs and tells her he is going into the

forest to see if he can catch some rabbits.

'Rabbits? Why would you want to catch rabbits?'

'Well, rabbits are a great source of protein. And if I can catch one, I can eat for a day or two.'

'My dad showed me a picture of a rabbit once. It looked really fluffy. Cute. Sweet, even.'

Ryan smiles and tells her she needs to stay indoors. 'I'll be back soon. But remember, if anything happens, I want you to hide, okay?' he says.

Ami agrees and tells him to be safe.

Ryan walks out of the door and closes it behind him. He then walks into the forest. In the depths of the wood, Ryan looks for few good spots and locates animal marks. He finds some good sticks and grabs some rope from his backpack. He ties the rope and sticks into a rabbit trap, and places it in a few spots he can see rabbit markings. Since he needs to wait, he walks around the forest, seeing if he can maybe find a rabbit or maybe a fox, or something he can just shoot.

An hour later, he is empty handed, and so he

decides to wait one more hour before checking the traps. He walks through the forest and then stumbles across a very big but low-hanging tree. He decides to climb into the tree and rest for a while. Enjoying the peace as he lays in the tree, time quickly flies and, soon enough, the sun going down. Ryan stretches himself and climbs out of the tree, and then walks over to the rabbit traps, but he finds it empty. 'Damn,' he curses to himself, and starts to walk back in the direction of the cabin.

When he arrives at the cabin, Ami is nowhere to be seen. He calls her name and then sees Ami coming from a different room. He asks what she was doing, and she tells him she heard someone so she was hiding.

'Ah okay, it was just me,' says Ryan.

Ryan tells her that he was not able to catch anything and so he will have to open his last can of beans. He tells Ami that if she could put a pan on the fire, he will get some wood for the fireplace.

'Sure,' says Ami, and she walks over to the stove.

Ryan walks outside and grabs a few logs of

wood. 'The logs are way too big,' he says to himself. 'We need an axe. Perhaps there's one in the barn.' He walks over to the barn and looks around. Sure enough, there he finds an axe and takes it with him. He chops up some wood and takes it into the cabin. He throws it in an old fireplace, together with some newspapers, and lights it up.

He asks Ami, 'How is the food going?'

'I think it's almost done,' she replies.

Ryan walks over to Ami. He looks at the beans and sees that they are indeed almost done.

'I did not know you could cook?' he says.

'Yes, my dad taught me. He taught me a lot of things'

'Like what?' Ryan asks.

'Well, when he created me I already knew a lot of things, like how to speak, how to read and how to walk. He told me that humans do not know how to do those things when they are born so I guess I was lucky. He taught me on how to keep my room clean and how to cook dinner. He taught me on how to take care of myself or other people, just in case anyone ever got hurt.'

Ryan smiles and looks at the food. 'I think the beans are done,' he says.

Ami picks up a plate and serves the food. She gives it to Ryan. With a smile on her face, she says 'Bon appetite!'

Ryan laughs and takes the plate and walks over to the couch. Ami sits next to him, and they start to talk.

'Ami, can I ask you something?'

'Sure. What do you want to know?'

'Well, I have been wondering. How do you keep running? Don't you need some sort of power supply like the other bots?'

'My body works just like yours. I have a heart that transports fluid through my body. And it will keep me running forever.'

'Wow. It's amazing what your dad did. He didn't only create a bot; he created life. I'm still trying to wrap my head around how it can happen that you have emotions. I just can't seem to understand it.'

Ami smiles and says, 'Even I do not know how it happened. I have felt emotions since the moment

I was created. At first, everything felt so weird. I did not know what it was. But after a while, the emotions just started to come out. One night, my dad was really angry about something and I got scared. He started to throw things around the room, and I asked him to please stop. I told him I was scared. He looked at me with so much surprise. The next day, he put me in that room and we started to talk for many hours, day in and day out.'

Ryan nods thoughtfully.

'Ryan, can I ask you something?'

'Sure,' he responds.

'Have you ever been in love?'

'Wow. Where did that come from?'

'I'm sorry. I didn't mean to offend you. It's just that the book I was reading kept talking about love. But I do not know how that feels.'

Ryan looks down to the ground and, with a sad expression on his face, starts to talk about how he used to have a girlfriend that he loved very much, but she died in the first year of the attacks. He relays how they fled the city early and wanted to go to my parents' cabin so that they could stay low for a while until the whole thing blew over, but on their way they ended up in a traffic jam so they had to walk. It was not long before they were out in the open, and that was when they came across some KBs.

'KBs?' Ami asks.

'That's what we call the bots that got infected by the virus,' says Ryan. 'Anyway, it all happened so fast. We came across a few KBs and they started shooting at us. We started to run but my girlfriend got shot in the leg. I tried to get her up but the KBs drew closer, and my girlfriend kept telling me to go. To leave her there. I tried to lift her but, before I knew it, she was hit again, this time in her chest. It did not take long before she stopped breathing. I didn't know what to do. I panicked so I ran. I ran in a different direction to my parents, and that was the last time I saw them. I've been on the run ever since.' Ryan wipes a few tears from his face.

'I'm so sorry that she died. I should never have brought that up. Please forgive me.'

'It's okay. It happened a long time ago.'

'Listen, it's getting late. We have a big day tomorrow so I should get some sleep.'

'What are we going to do tomorrow?' Ami asks.

'I will tell you in the morning. Can you please wake me up tomorrow as soon as the sun comes up?'

'Okay. Have a good night's rest.' Ami walks over to the closet and picks out another book, and again she starts reading.

Ryan makes himself comfortable in the couch. He rolls over and, still with tears in his eyes, he slowly falls to sleep.

The next morning, he wakes up to the smell of food. He opens his eyes and sees that Ami is baking something. He stands up and walks over to her, and sees that she is making eggs.

'Where did you get the eggs?' he asks.

'There are some chickens at the back,' she smiles. 'My dad always loved eggs so I thought you might also like them.'

'This is great, thank you! It's been well over a year since I last had an omelette!'

Ami puts the omelette on a plate and gives it to Ryan. He sits on the couch and starts to eat.

'So where will we be going today?' Ami asks.

'Well, once I'm done eating, we'll pack our things and head to the sewers. There were rumours about a small resistance group over there, and I think we will be a lot safer down there then here in the open.'

With a frightened voice, Ami replies, 'But what about me? What if they find out that I'm not human?'

'It will be okay. With your wig and dress, they won't find out. Once we are there, we'll see if we can make it work without them finding out you are an AI. I won't leave you alone.' He smiles at her. She smiles in response but with a bit of uncertainty in her eyes.

Ryan starts to pack his stuff and asks Ami if she is ready to go. They then leave the cabin and begin their walk in the direction of the forest.

The sun has just come up, but already it is very warm outside. The rays filter through the trees. The birds' song can be heard as the wind carries the sweetness through the trees.

'Everything feels so peaceful like this. You

wouldn't think what a mess this world is in,' Ryan comments.

'I wish I could have seen the world before all of this happened,' Amy sighs.

They both enjoy the peace for a moment, and then Ami asks, 'So how do you know in which direction we need to go?'

'I met a guy a few weeks back,' Ryan continues. 'He told me that if I would keep walking north, eventually I would see a lot of pipes laying out above the ground. Once we have found those, all we have to do is to follow them and then they should lead us to an entrance.'

After walking for a while, Ami asks Ryan if he thinks they are almost there.

'I don't know. I might be able to see more if I climb up one of the trees.'

Ryan looks around and sees a large pine tree with an abundance of branches sticking out. He throws his backpack in front of the tree and tells Ami to wait where she is. He then begins to climb into the tree and, when ten feet high, he starts to look around.

It is difficult to see, but it looks like that there are some open spots in the distance. He carefully climbs down but, at one of the last few branches, he slips and falls. He lands on his back, and the dust on the ground flies up and around him. Ami quickly runs to him and asks if he is alright.

'Yeah, I'm fine,' he laughs, embarrassed. 'But this is going to hurt for the next few days!' he says. He slowly stands up, grabs his backpack, and then they continue walking towards the open spots.

After another thirty minutes, they see a few small pipes protruding up from under the ground. As Ryan was instructed, they start to follow the pipes and, not long after, they come across some bigger pipes. They look badly damaged, with large holes gaping through them. It looks almost like some of them have been blown up.

Ryan looks around and, in the distance, he sees another big pipe—big enough for a person to fit in.

They walk over to the pipe, and Ryan finds a spot where there is a hole big enough to get in. He tells Ami that he does not know what will be on the other side and to stay close to him.

He climbs in the pipe and then grabs Ami's hand to help her to get in too. It's dark and smells bad. Ryan takes his lighter from his backpack and allows the flame to burn. They then start to walk through the tunnel created by the large pipe, and not too long after, they stumble upon a large metal frame, behind which seem to be underground sewers. Ryan tells Ami to hold the lighter, and he tries to open the metal frame. It is stuck and struggles to open, but after a few kicks, it comes lose.

'Okay, I'm going to lift this up, then you need to crawl under very quickly and try to hold it for me from the other side,' Ryan tells Ami. 'Do you think you can you do it?'

'Of course,' Ami replies with a smile in her voice.

'Okay, on the count of three. Ready? One, two, three. Go!'

Ryan lifts up the gate and Ami crawls through it. She then holds up the gate from the other side, and Ryan quickly makes his way through and into the sewers.

CHAPTER 3

THE SEWERS

Ryan and Ami walk through the sewer. Luckily, the stench is not nearly as noticeable since it has been out of service for so long. They walk through a wide, open-mouthed tunnel. The ground, walls and upper dome are moist, and drops of water can be seen and heard as they fall from the ceiling, creating puddles on the ground.

After walking for a few minutes, Ami hears a sound. 'What was *that*?' she asks.

'What? I didn't hear anything,' says Ryan.

They stop, and Ryan listens closely. He hears what sounds like people, all walking, in the distance.

'Maybe it's the resistance,' Ami suggests.

Ryan tells Ami he's not sure. 'But I do know we need to go carefully. For all we know, it could be a

KB. Or worse, many.'

They walk a few more feet until they come to a crossing. Ryan hears the noise getting louder, and it is heading in their direction. He quickly grabs Ami by her arm and pulls her around the corner. He pulls out his gun and gets ready to shoot, just in case needed. He waits for the sound to come closer, but then, all of a sudden, the sound stops.

Ryan hesitates and carefully looks around the corner. It is dark, but the faint outline of a person can be seen standing just a few feet away from them, his back to them.

Ryan looks at Ami and gestured for her to stay where she is. He turns and walks around the corner.

All of a sudden, there is a big KB standing right in front of him, his chest glowing bright red. The KB grabs Ryan's troth and throws him a few feet away and to the ground. Ryan drops his gun not far from Ami, and in that split second, he can do nothing but watch as Ami grabs the gun.

The KB comes round the corner and looks at Ami. She closes her eyes and starts to shoot.

The first bullet enters in at his arm, whilst the

53

second travels into his shoulder.

The KB quickly comes closer, but Ami hits him in his chest. The KB falls to the ground and stops moving. She then fires two more rounds into the wall until the clip is empty. She slowly opens her eyes, and looks down to see the robot lay in front of her. Shocked, she does not move but merely keeps staring at the KB.

Ryan slowly comes closer and tells her that it is over. He slowly takes the gun from Ami's hands and puts it away in his back pocket. He sits in front of Ami and tells her that she saved his life. 'If you hadn't done that, we both would have been killed,' he tells her.

Ami shifts her eyes to Ryan and she gives him a hug. 'I'm so glad you're okay,' she says in a high-pitched voice.

Ryan looks Ami in the eyes and he tells her that these bots are evil, that they do not care about life and do not have emotions. He tells her they merely eliminate everything that lives.

Ami nods, and Ryan helps her up. Ryan picks up his backpack that had been thrown away by the

KB. He pulls it out of the dirty water; it stinks.

They start to walk. Ami is behind Ryan but holds his arm. She is scared, even though she won't admit it.

They walk north for a few minutes, but then they stumble across a room inside the sewers. It looks almost like an old generator room, but you can see that there people used to live there; there are chairs, mattresses and clothes. There are tables with old, empty bottles of water, but the worst of all is the decomposing dead on the floor.

Ryan and Ami walk through the room. Ami asks what happened, and Ryan replies, 'They probably got overrun by KBs. I wouldn't look at them too much.'

They walk over to some tables that still have some cans of food on them. Ryan tells Ami that now they're here it can't hurt to look around and see if they can find anything useful. They split up and walk around the room. Ami finds two bottles of water and takes them back to Ryan. She gives Ryan the bottles and continues to look around. After a few more minutes, they hear something.

Ryan quickly tells Ami to come to him, and they look around for a place to hide.

It is a large, open room, and so all Ryan can think off is picking up one of the tables and putting it on its side. They hide behind the table. Ryan picks out his gun, and they wait whilst listening to the sounds of footsteps moving closer and closer.

Ryan aims his gun at the tunnel and, not too soon after, three KBs turn round the corner. Ryan quickly ducks back behind the table and makes a quiet signal to Ami with his finger. He tries to sit up straight, but at the worst possible moment, the cans in his backpack hit the ground. *Shit!* thinks Ryan.

He waits for a few seconds longer, but then he hears that the KBs make themselves ready to shoot. Whenever a KB starts to shoot, you can hear a slight clicking noise as they charge up their gun.

Ryan quickly jumps up from behind the table and, before the KBs have charged their guns, he shoots one of them in the chest. It was a lucky shot, and the KB falls down at the first hit. The other KBs start to shoot, and Ryan quickly ducks behind the table again. Without looking, he aims his gun above the table and starts shooting. He hits another KB, which falls down on the ground with a loud noise. Ryan then quickly reloads his gun, but he cannot find a good moment to stick his head out to aim. He looks at Ami and sees that she is frightened for her life, sitting with her hands in front of her face. He looks at his backpack and there sees one of the cans of food lay on the ground. He gets an idea and he picks up the can of food, and then gets ready to shoot once again.

He throws the can of food roughly in the direction of the KB, causing the KB to be distracted; in that split second, the KB looks at the can and Ryan jumps out and shoots the KB in the head and a second time in the chest. The KB falls down. The last sound they hear is the empty bullet casing falling onto the concrete.

Then everything falls silent.

Ryan takes a moment to acknowledge what just happened, and he then directs his focus to Ami.

He sits behind the table and tells her it's over. Ami looks up and asks 'Are they dead?'

'Yes, don't worry. They can't hurt us anymore.'

Ryan picks up his backpack and puts everything that fell out of it back inside. He stands up and stretches his hand out to Ami. She takes his hand and he pulls her up. She looks at the KBs, a sad look in her eyes.

Ryan tells her he thinks they are almost there. They start to walk again in the direction of the tunnel. They walk for a good twenty minutes before reaching another crossing. Ami asks which way they need to go. Ryan takes a green army compass from his backpack and states they are still going north. He tells Ami that they need to go left.

They walk into the left tunnel, and there they come across a room that seems to have a few smaller rooms in and around it. They walk round the corner and there, out of nowhere, they bump into two KBs standing just a few feet away. Within a split-second, Ryan grabs his gun and shoots one of the KBs. He takes Ami's arm, and quickly they run back and hide round the corner in one of the smaller rooms. Ryan signs that she needs to be quiet.

They are sat in a pitch-black black room. Ryan looks at Ami and, to his amazement, he can see her chest glowing bright blue. It's her heart, he realises:

it glows bright blue and he can see it beating.

Even in a situation like this, Ryan feels suddenly calm and focused.

Ami looks down with a shy but also frightened face.

A few minutes pass and nothing happens. Ryan carefully looks round the corner to see if the KB is anywhere to be seen, but, thankfully, it looks like it has passed them.

They slowly step out of the room and Ryan asks Ami if she is okay. 'Yes, but my dress got all dirty,' she says.

'Don't worry, I'm sure that when we get to the resistance we can find a new dress for you.'

'Thanks,' says Ami, and gives Ryan a hug.

They continue their journey and, after walking for about half an hour, they see a big gate made from scrap metal and other debris. Ryan takes Ami aside and tells her that she needs to stay close and act like a human. 'Whatever happens never reveal that you are an AI, okay?' Ami agrees, and Ryan and Ami start to walk towards the gate.

They approach the gate and, suddenly, a big

light turns on and points at them. They look around them and see that there are countless dead KBs lay on the ground. Two guards come out of the gates with automatic rifles, which they point at Ryan and Ami. The light shines in Ryan and Ami's faces, and they can hardly see a thing.

CHAPTER 4

THE RESISTANCE

Ryan and Ami stand in front of the gate. The two guards come closer, and one of them yells with a deep voice. 'Identify yourselves!'

Ami backs away and, with a scared look on her face, stands close behind Ryan, holding his arm.

'Don't shoot, we are human!' says Ryan. 'We are looking for the resistance.'

'What do you need the resistance for?' the guard asks.

'We want to join them. We want a safe place to live and to help out wherever we can,' Ryan replies urgently.

The guard comes closer and stands right in front of Ryan. He is wearing a SWAT uniform and has a gas mask over his face. He tells Ryan that they are at the right address. He grabs Ryan by his arm, whilst the other guard grabs Ami.

The gate opens and they walk through it. All too quickly, the gate closes again and the guard tells them to stand still and spread their arms. He inspects Ryan for any weapons and finds his gun. 'You cannot bring any weapons in until you have spoken to the boss,' the guard advises. He then walks over to Ami and, when he wants to Inspect her, Ryan tells him, 'She does not have any weapons. Can't you see that?'

The guard tells Ryan it is standard procedure.

Ami looks frightened when the guard comes closer. Ryan holds his breath as the guard starts to inspect Ami; he is afraid they might realise she is an AI. But luckily, the guard is gentle and does not actually touch her; he only feels her dress to see if she has any weapons concealed beneath the fabric.

'They're clean,' he calls out.

The guards then guide Ryan and Ami through a wide hallway with another large metal door at the end. The guard knocks at the door three times, and the door opens.

They find themselves in a very big room, filled with tents and houses made from debris and scrap metal. It looks almost like a little town. They start to walk through the town and can see a lot of people. There are men and women, but also children. Most of them look dirty and worn out. Everyone looks very serious, sad and hopeless.

They walk past a few tents and see a pregnant woman with ripped clothes sitting on the floor. She asks if they have any water for her. Ryan wants to stop to give her some, but the guards won't allow him.

There are more and more people leaving their tents and houses to see what's going on. Ryan notices that Ami is starting to get scared, and so he looks back at Ami and tells her that everything will be all right. After walking for a few minutes, they find themselves at a wall with a few doors in it. The guards open up one the doors and tell Ryan and Ami to go through. They step through and there they end up in a small room with only a table and three chairs.

The room is concrete and the door is metal; it

almost feels like an interrogation room.

The guards tell them to stay put until the boss comes.

Ryan and Ami sit down, and the guards walk outside, locking the door behind them.

Ryan tells Ami that everything will be okay. 'Just act the same as always, but this time act like you already know the world,' says Ryan, a smile on his face.

A few hours pass, and Ryan begins to grow tired and impatient. The chair is uncomfortable and there is no real place to lay their heads. He begins to get irritated but, just when he wants to walk over to the door to ask how long it is going to take, two guards enter. They tell Ryan to sit down and that there is someone who wants to speak to them.

Shortly after, a big man walks in. He wears clean jeans with a shirt and a blue jacket. He looks like a high-profile guy. The guards tell Ryan that this is the boss of the resistance. He slowly walks over to Ryan and Ami, and sits in the chair opposite. He takes a large Cuban cigar from his pocket and lights it up. He takes his time and makes himself comfortable, then asks, with a deep and authoritative voice, 'So, what brings you here?'

'We are here to join the resistance. We want to help you in your fight and have everyone be able to return to a safe place to stay,' says Ryan.

With an irritated face, the boss says, 'Haven't you seen this place? There is no fight. It's a losing battle. We once were the resistance, but now all we are trying to do is survive.'

'There must be some resistance left? We can't give up now. We came a long way to find you guys!'

The boss focuses his attention on Ami. With a creepy voice he says, 'Well, aren't you a pretty girl?'

Ryan puts his arm in front of Ami to signal the boss to back off. 'Listen, I will do whatever job you have for me. All we want is a safe place to stay,' says Ryan.

The boss looks at Ryan and says, 'Okay. We have a few small teams that still do small operations to gather supplies and to keep the perimeter safe. Do you know how to fight?'

'Yes. If I didn't know I wouldn't be here.' Sarcasm fills his voice.

'Good,' says the boss, and again focuses his attention on Ami. 'And what are we going to do with you? I'm sure you are not as capable of fighting are you?'

Ami looks at the ground and, with a frightened voice, says, 'No. Ryan is the one who has protected me this entire time.'

'Well, I guess you can help out the other women with cooking dinner, washing clothes and taking care of everyone.' The boss takes a deep breath and tells Ryan and Ami that he will see if he has a place for them to stay. 'The guards will tell you where you need to go. In the evening, I will send someone that tells you where you can sleep for the night,' he continues.

'Thank you!' says Ryan with excitement.

The boss stands up and walks out of the door. One of the guards walks over to Ryan and tells him he has been assigned to team SG3. The team will go out for a supply run tomorrow morning. Until that time, Ryan is told he can have a look around and then the guards will return to show him where he is to stay for the night.

The guards leave, leaving Ryan and Ami to stand alone in the room. Ryan takes a deep breath. 'Well, I think this is it then. We will see how it goes from here.' He asks Ami if she wants to have a look around whilst waiting.

'Sure,' agrees Ami.

'Okay. Let's go.' Together, Ryan and Ami walk out the door.

They start to walk through the town-like place, with its individual rows, forming streets. It is a dirty place; exactly would you would expect from a sewer.

The surrounding area is comparable to the slums in third-world countries.

By now, almost everything is better than being outside and always needing to be prepared to fight.

Ryan and Ami walk around for a while, during which time they see a lot of people who look sick and hopeless. Ami starts to feel depressed as a result of looking at all those poor people who are just trying to survive. She asks Ryan if they can stop walking around and if they can go to where the people sleep.

Ryan looks around and sees a guard standing

on a corner of a house that is no more than a few metal frames making up the wall. He walks over to the guard and tells him that they are just new and they are wondering if the boss already has found a place for them to stay. The guard looks at them with an irritated look in his eyes. He then takes a radio from his pocket and asks the other guards if anyone knows where the new guys can stay. He gets a reply that they have been assigned to Section B1, Seat 34. He tells them to follow the signs, and points at a few wooden planks with written on them.

Ryan and Ami walk to the signs and see that Section B is close by. They follow the signs to Section B, where they start walking through the street that is made up out of small tents. Most of the tents are dirty or ripped open. They start to walk, and each tent has a number written on the front of it on the concrete floor. They arrive at number 34, which is a small two-person yellow tent. Luckily, the tent still looks somewhat intact.

Ryan puts his bag in the tent, and then Ami says, 'I liked the cabin more.'

'Give it some time. I'm sure things will turn

around. I also expected more of this place but we will see how it goes,' says Ryan.

There are two folding chairs on the ground next to the tent. Ryan picks up the chairs and unfolds them. He sits in one and Ami sits in the other.

Everything falls silent for a moment; Ryan looks disappointed with the place.

Ami asks if everything is alright.

'Yes, everything is okay. I just expected more. But at least we're safe.'

'It is like you said: if we don't like it after a while, we can leave, right?'

'That's true. We will see how it goes,' says Ryan.

Ryan looks in his backpack and takes out his last can of food. There is no fire to warm it, so he just opens the can, takes a spoon from his backpack and starts to eat from the tin.

It is very silent during dinner this time; normally, Ryan and Ami would talk for hours, but they do not feel safe talking at the camp.

Ryan finishes his food and tells Ami it is

getting late. 'Why don't we call it a day and see how it goes tomorrow?' he suggests.

Ryan tells Ami to stay in the tent until he wakes up. They stand up and crawl into the tent. They close the entrance and make themselves comfortable. 'Goodnight,' says Ryan, and he rolls over and slowly falls to sleep.

Ami lies next to him and just stares at the tent ceiling. She has the look on her face that she has a lot of emotions bottled up.

The following morning, they are woken up by a speaker blasting through the room. It sounds like the boss, and he says 'It is eight o' clock, people. Wake up and we will see you at your posts in thirty minutes.'

Ami and Ryan slowly wake up and walk out of their tent. They see other people leaving their tents, left and right, and everyone starts walking to their posts.

'Okay, it looks like nobody is getting breakfast so I think we will just follow the signs to our post,' says Ryan.

'The guard told me you will have to stay with

the women today and cook dinner.'

With a frightened voice, Ami says, 'So you are going to leave me? What if they find out I'm not human and they hurt me?'

'I know that you are scared but, believe me, if you keep acting like you did all this time then everything will be just fine. Just don't talk too much and never mention that you are not human. I will be back in a few hours.'

Ryan and Ami start to walk through the street and see a few signs saying *kitchen*, *operations* and *bunker*. They follow the signs and they arrive at the kitchen. The kitchen is made up of a big tent with a few tables.

By the looks of it, there is not a lot of food, and there are only a few women standing around, cutting vegetables, opening cans of food and cleaning dishes. Ryan stops just in front of the kitchen and tells Ami this is the place and that she needs to stay. 'Just do what the other women say. You like cooking so you will be fine,' says Ryan.

Ryan wants to let go of Ami's hand, but she does not let go of his. 'I'm scared,' she says.

Ryan looks her in the eyes and, with a friendly voice, says, 'Don't be. I won't let anything happen to you and I will be back soon, and then we can be together for the rest of the day.'

Ami smiles and, still with some hesitation, let's go of his arm. Ryan starts to walk in the direction of *operations* and, when looking back, he sees Ami standing in the middle of the street, looking after him. He waves one last time and then walks round the corner.

Ryan arrives at *operations* and sees a few men standing around a table filled with guns and ammunition. He walks up to them and tells them that he is new and has been sent to assist. One man with a clipboard walks forward. He is dressed in a SWAT uniform and has an assault rifle hanging at his back and a big knife strapped to his chest.

'What's your name, boy?' he asks.

'My name is Ryan, Sir.'

'Ah, Ryan. t boss told me you were coming. You will be going on a supply run with me and the boys. My name is Brian. over there is Paul, Daniel, David and Jack.'

Ryan shakes hands with the guys and introduces himself.

'Do you know how to shoot?' asks Brian.

'Of course, although the guns are a whole lot bigger here then I'm used to. But I have shot with an assault rifle before.'

'Good,' says Brian. He walks over to the table and picks up an assault rifle—a G36C. He hands it to Ryan and tells him that they do not have a lot of bullets so, if he has to shoot, to make every shot count. Ryan also gets handed a bulletproof vest, which he puts straight on.

The rest of the men start to gear up and load their rifles.

Brian asks if everyone if ready, and then they start to walk through the street.

They walk through a big metal double door and arrive in one of the smaller tunnels. 'There is an exit to the outside not far from here. It is about one mile to the village. There have been no signs of KBs for a while now, so we will go in quick, grab what we find and get out.'

After walking for a few minutes, the group

arrives at a side tunnel. Everyone needs to crouch to fit in. They walk through the tunnel and arrive at a large metal frame. One of the guys lifts up the frame, and everyone quickly climbs through. They hold up the frame from the outside, and the last guy climbs through.

They stand in the middle of the forest again; everyone takes a deep breath of fresh air.

'One of the benefits of being on operations: we can enjoy some fresh air from time to time! Too bad we need to risk out lives for it,' comments Brian.

They all start to walk behind Brian and through to a small rocky path.

'Okay, guys. It's just one mile to the village. Even though KBs normally do not come here, I want you to stay focused and keep your eyes open,' commands Brian.

It is morning, and the sun shines low again. Most of the men wear sunglasses, but Ryan needs to shield his eyes with his hand so that he is able to see everything.

After walking for a while, they arrive at the village. They stop in front of the village and sit behind a big log. One of the guys grabs binoculars and checks if the coast is clear. 'It looks like a ghost town,' he muses.

'Okay, keep your eyes open and your guns ready,' says Brian.

They start to slowly walk towards the village. They walk past a few houses whilst sticking close to the walls.

'Our best bet is the shopping centre not far from here. This village was overrun in the very beginning, so there are still a lot of supplies left.'

They arrive at a corner; everything looks clear. They run across the street and into one of the stores. They see that there is still quite a bit of food left—all the fresh food rotted long ago, but there are still enough cans of food to feed thirty people for a week.

'Wow. Looks like we have a winner! I think we will have to do two runs to get everything,' says Brian.

Everyone starts to put cans in their backpack. Whilst everyone is packing their bags, one of the guys says he can hear something. Everyone falls quiet, and again they listen. They hear what sounds like someone walking around at the front of the store.

Everyone drops down low, and one of the guys slowly goes to the window and looks outside. Ryan can see him looking round to see if there is anyone, but then, all of a sudden, the guy is shot through the head. Immediately, Brian calls out to take cover. Everything falls silent again for a few seconds, but then they hear the sound of guns warming up.

Everyone is familiar with the sound, and they grab their guns, ready to shoot.

There are three KBs, and they rush into the store and start shooting at every living thing they see. Within the first few seconds, two of the men have been shot and have fallen to the ground. Everyone starts to shoot at the KBs. Ryan shoots one of the KBs and it falls down. Brian and another guy take care of the other two KBs. Not long after all KBs are down, another two rush into the store. Brian yells out that everyone needs to go to the back, and so they quickly run through a back door and find themselves in the back yard of the store. They quickly run past the wall and knock over a fence.

The KBs come running after them, and Ryan looks back and shoots at one.

'Nice shot,' says Brian as they run. They run through another backyard and find the entrance to another house.

Brian tells Ryan to get the door while he and another guy hold off the other KB. Ryan starts to kick against the door and after a few tries the door breaks open. Everyone runs inside the house and immediately run through the kitchen and into the living room. Ryan runs to the front door and kicks it down in one go. Everyone quickly runs into the street and starts to run back in the direction of the forest.

Two KBs are behind them so, as the men run, they keep shooting back at the KBs. Ryan manages to hit one, and it falls over, tripping the other KB as it does so. Paul has been shot in his arm and is unable to shoot, and so Ryan takes a quick few seconds to stop running, aims, and with a well-placed shot, he shoots down the last KB.

By now, they have reached the border of the forest, and quickly they jump over a fallen tree and hide behind its trunk to take a few deep breaths.

Paul looks over the tree to see if there are any more KBs coming behind them, but it looks like the coast is clear.

'Nice shooting,' Brian tells Ryan. 'We've lost three good men out there,' he says with a sad expression on his face. 'We owe it to the families to recover the bodies when it's safe to do so.'

Brian asks Paul how he is doing, and Paul replies, 'Nothing that won't heal.'

Brian asks Ryan and Paul if they at least got some supplies.

'I've got about ten cans,' says Ryan.

'I got eight,' says Paul.

'Well at least that's something. I think it's best if we go back to the base,' Brian suggests.

They slowly stand up and start to walk back to the tunnel entrance. It is a silent walk, with everyone quiet and thinking of the fallen men. The silence helps them all to accept and come to terms with what happened.

After walking for a while, they arrive at the tunnel entrance and lift up the metal frame. They step inside the tunnel and walk back to operations. They arrive back at the tables where they met, and lay down their gear. Brian walks over to Ryan and tells him he did a good job, especially considering it was the first time.

'Thanks. I only wish we were able to save the other men,' says Ryan.

'Yes, they were good men. Tomorrow we'll send out a scout to see if the coast is clear and, if so, we will go back and recover their bodies. It's the least we can do.'

Ryan gives Brian a hand, and they start walking in the direction of where he left Ami. Soon enough, Ryan arrives at the kitchen, but he cannot see her. He asks one of the women if they have seen her, but they do not look at him and, with what almost sounds like a frightened voice, they say that she walked away about an hour ago and they have not seen her since.

Ryan is surprised and tries to think of a reason for why she would do that.

Maybe she went back to the tent, he thinks. He starts to walk in the direction of the tent and, on his way, he asks a few people if they have seen a girl around 25 years old wearing a red dress. Some people say that they have not seen her, but most people ignore Ryan and just walk away. Ryan thinks everything is very strange, and he is starting to get worried. He arrives at the tent and looks inside, but she is not there. He takes his backpack and starts to walk around the surrounding area, but Ami is nowhere to be seen.

After walking around for well over an hour, Ryan decides to go to the boss's office to ask if he knows where she is. He walks up to one of the guards at the corner of the street and asks him where he can find the office of the boss.

'If you walk down this road and then turn left, you'll see a concrete rooms imbedded into the tunnel. Just ask one of the guards there where the boss is,' says the guard.

Ryan follows the guard's instructions and arrives at the rooms. There he is met by two heavily armed guards standing in front of a door that leads into one of the rooms. He walks up to the guards and asks if he can speak to the boss. One guard steps forward and tells Ryan to wait where he is whilst the other guard knocks on the door and calls out, 'There's someone to see you, boss.'

A voice booms, 'Let him in.'

The guards step aside and Ryan walks through the door. He finds a fairly large concrete room with a simple desk and a comfortable chair. He sees the boss sitting relaxed in his chair smoking a cigar. Ryan needs to crouch down because of the smoke hanging in the room; there is no ventilation whatsoever, but the boss seems to be fine with that.

Ryan walks in and asks him if he has seen Ami.

'Who?' he asks.

'The girl I was with.'

The boss has a mean expression on his face and tells Ryan, 'She must be walking around here somewhere.' His tone drips with sarcasm. 'If I see her, I will let you know.'

Ryan does not trust the boss one bit, and he walks out of the office feeling irritated. He heads back onto the street. He starts to walk around again in a final attempt to find Ami. As he is walking through a small alley that might only fit one person at a time through it, he walks by a tent and there he hears two men talking. He hears them saying something about a girl. Ryan stops walking and silently moves closer to the tent.

He hears one of the guys saying that the guards recently found a girl that turned out to be a KB.

'They can make themselves look like humans. How can we ever be safe?' asks the guy in the tent.

'What happened to her?' asks the other guy.

'All I know is they took her to the bunker. They'll probably inspect her better since this is the first time they've seen a KB dressed like a human.'

Ryan feels chills run over him. He is scared, and quickly runs through the alley and onto a bigger street. He looks around him and he can remember seeing a few signs this morning that gave directions to the bunker. He walks through the street and comes across the signs that point East, and detail: *In a case of emergency, follow these signs to the bunker.*

Ryan runs through the street in the direction of the bunker. He keeps following the signs and, after a few minutes, arrives at a big metal door in one of the walls. The bunker.

The door must be two metres high, and Ryan sees a group of five guards standing around it. They all are wearing bulletproof vests and are equipped with machine guns.

Ryan plays it cool and, with a relaxed walk, approaches the bunker door. The guards see him coming and, when Ryan comes closer, they walk up to him and. with threatening voices, tell him the area is off-limits.

'Okay, sorry. I was just looking around.' Ryan says, and he slowly backs away.

Surrounding the bunker, there are a few concrete rooms that look almost like houses. Ryan walks up to one of the houses and leans against the wall. He looks at the bunker. *How the hell do I get in there?* he wonders. He looks around him to see if there are any other ways into the bunker, but the only place he can see is the heavily guarded metal door. Then he hears something coming from the house he is standing against. It sounds like metal objects falling to the ground.

He looks around him to see if anyone is watching him, and when the coast is clear, he slowly opens the door to the house. Ryan finds himself in a very small hallway. He takes only three steps and arrives at another door.

The sound gets louder, and Ryan gets ready to open the door. He is sick and tired of being careful, and so he grabs his gun. He slams open the door and ends up in a small kitchen. Right in front of him there is a man cooking dinner. He looks over and sees Ryan standing with his gun.

The man reacts quickly and grabs his knife and comes running at Ryan with the intention of stabbing him. Without thinking, Ryan aims his gun and fires two shots. He watches as the man falls down right in front of him, and it takes Ryan a few seconds to realise what just happened. It shocks Ryan that he has just killed an innocent man who was just protecting his home. He runs to the man who is gasping for air. 'I didn't mean to shoot you… It was a reflex,' Ryan tries to explain, his voice frightened.

In the last few seconds of the guy's life, all he can do is give Ryan an angry look.

It does not take long for the man to and, a few

seconds after getting shot, he dies in Ryan arms.

'Shit, Shit, Shit!' Ryan says aloud, blinking back tears of anger and frustration. 'I fucking hate this world!' He leaves the man on the floor and walks back to the door, and listens carefully to try to establish whether anyone has heard the shots. Luckily, after waiting for thirty seconds, no one comes.

Ryan quickly walks over to the guy and lifts up his upper body. He drags the body into a corner and leaves it there. He walks through the room and sees the knife the guy dropped. He picks it up and looks at it. It is a normal chef's knife, but it has some blood splatters on it. He looks around the room and, to his surprise, sees what looks like a food elevator that can go down.

'But the floor is concrete…' Ryan muses to himself. 'Where does that elevator lead to?'

Ryan decides that he needs to get out quickly, and so he walks over to the elevator and throws out some dishes that were standing in it. He climbs into the elevator; he barely fits so he has to leave his backpack in the house. He presses a green button that is outside the elevator, and slowly, the elevator begins to move down and everything gets dark.

CHAPTER 5

THE ESCAPE

Ryan arrives at the bottom of the elevator. He climbs out and finds himself in a small storage room. The walls are made from a rough grey concrete. Ryan looks around and sees a few metal storage shelves with food lined on them.

He wants to pick his backpack and stack it with food for later, but then he realises he had to leave it behind in the kitchen. 'Shit,' he murmurs to himself.

He walks to the door; it is a simple metal door. In that moment, as he goes to open the door, he hears some voices outside; it sounds like two men having a random conversation about gambling. Ryan listens closely and establishes that the men are just a few feet away from the door. He looks through the keyhole and sees one of them with his back to him. Ryan holds the knife ready to attack, and opens the door slightly. He sticks his head through and sees two guards talking a few feet away on the corner of another hallway. Luckily, they are facing away, with their backs to Ryan.

He sees an opportunity.

He slowly crawls outside the room and, without making a sound, he approaches the guards. He takes a deep breath and then jumps up, running at the guards, and quickly stabs one in his back. The sound of a spine cracking echoes, with the guard almost instantly dying. Before the other guard can even consider what just happened, Ryan turns to him and slices his throat. The guard falls down, desperately gasping for air. It does not take long before everything falls quiet.

Ryan has tears in his eyes, brought on by what he has just done. He is covered in blood, but he shakes off his emotions and looks around to see where he needs to go next. He sees that, on the walls, they have spray-painted arrows with text. He sees one arrow that points to the entrance and two other arrows detailing the office and laboratory, pointing right. Ryan decides to walk in the direction of the office and laboratory. He walks through the hall and around the corner, but there he sees the office arrow pointing right and the laboratory arrow pointing left.

If they found out she's an AI, I'm almost sure they'd have taken her to the laboratory, he thinks.

He walks in the direction of the laboratory and stumbles across a white double-folding door. He slowly opens the door to find a more modern room; it looks a bit like a research lab, with almost everything white—the walls, the floor and the ceiling.

Ryan hears voices in the distance, and slowly he crouches down as he walks towards them. He sees a lot of doors and a few large windows in the wall. It looks like the entire area is divided into small rooms. He looks through one of the windows and sees an operating table, which is covered in blood. There are a lot of surgical tools laying around.

Ryan's heart starts to knock faster, and soon he is beginning to feel scared. He quickly walks over to the second window, and there he sees Ami lay on a metal table, strapped down, her mouth been taped shut. Ryan's heart skips a beat as he watches, tears springing to his eyes.

There are two men in doctors' uniforms in the room. It looks like they are preparing equipment and talking to one another about what to do with her. Ryan feels anger surge in him, and he takes out his gun. Quickly, he crawls underneath the window and walks around the corner into another hallway. There, he sees the door that leads into the room Ami is in.

He stands next to the door, takes a few deep breaths, and kicks in the door.

The doctors are startled and ask what he is doing there.

With anger deep in his voice, Ryan shouts, 'Back off! Stand against the wall!'

The doctors slowly put their hands up and back away.

Ryan runs over to Ami and, when he is about to unstrap her, he sees from the corner of his eye that one of the doctors has grabbed a gun that was hidden under one of the tables. Ryan quickly looks over and sees the doctor aiming at him. The doctor and Ryan shoot at one another at the same time. The doctor manages to shoot once before he is shot in the chest. Ryan is furious and looks at the other doctor.

'Please don't kill me!' pleads the doctor, but Ryan won't listen.

He takes a few steps towards the doctor, aims, and shoots him in the head.

He then returns to Ami and quickly unstraps her lose and takes the tape from her mouth.

All is silent for a moment as they look into each other's eyes. Ryan can see how terrified Ami is. He begins to feel a burning sensation in his shoulder, and, upon examination, realises he is bleeding. Apparently that doctor managed to shoot him in the shoulder but, thanks to the adrenalin, he had not felt it until now.

'You alright?' Ami asks in a soft voice.

'Yes, I'm fine. I'm so glad you're okay.'

Ami gives Ryan a hug and says, 'I'm so glad you came back for me. I was so scared.'

Ryan gets tears in his eyes again. He wipes

them away and pulls himself together. He tells Ami that they need to get out of here fast. 'It won't be long before they come to look at what is happening. This place is not safe anymore.'

He helps Ami off the table, takes out a Mag from his pocket, and reloads his gun. Together, they then walk outside the room and into the hallway. They walk back in the direction of the food elevator. They pass through the hallway and around the corner to where Ryan killed the two guards. There they see three guards standing over the dead bodies, attempting to figure out what happened.

Ryan makes one step too many and the guards hear it. They look over their shoulder and see Ryan and Ami. They grab their guns and immediately start to shoot.

Ryan quickly shoots back and hits one of the guards. He then pulls Ami around the corner and quickly they run into one of the operation rooms. Not long after, they hear a loud alarm sounding.

Ryan sets Ami down and tells her she needs to stay low.

'What are we going to do?' she asks.

'To be honest, I don't know. I think the only way to get through this is by shooting our way out.' He checks his pistol and sees that he has only nine bullets left. He breaks a window in the door and prepares for the guards to come around the corner at any second. To his luck, the guards did not know that he was in the room, and instead they run around the corner without caution.

Ryan starts to shoot at both of the guards. He manages to kill both of them with just one bullet each. He looks up and, to his surprise, sees there are no more guards coming. 'Okay. Now or never,' he says to Ami. He takes Ami's arm and they get up and quickly walk, but with caution, through the hall. They walk around the corner, and Ryan sees the door he came through that leads to the food elevator. They quickly run to the door and arrive in the room.

Ryan tells Ami to get in the food elevator. 'I will be right behind you,' he says.

Ami climbs in the food elevator and Ryan presses the button for it to go up.

Right at the moment the elevator goes up, Ryan

sees two more guards who come running around the corner. He walks to the door and shoots one of them. The guard falls over, and the other guard quickly jumps back behind the corner. He starts to shoot at Ryan from behind the corner, and Ryan is forced to take cover behind the wall. He desperately looks to see if the elevator is already back, and hears that it is coming down. He waits for the elevator to come down, and then he shoots his last few rounds in the direction of the guard and quickly climbs in. He presses the button and the elevator slowly goes up. He sees the guard coming out of cover and the guard shoots a few rounds at Ryan. Luckily, they all miss, and Ryan goes up with the elevator.

At the top, Ryan is back in the kitchen. He climbs out and quickly walks to the counter, where he picks up a wooden cutting board and blocks the elevator with it. He looks at Ami and sees that she is holding his backpack. Ryan grabs the backpack and tells Ami they need to find some clothes for her so that she can blend into the masses. He quickly runs into the living room in the hope of finding some clothes there. Ami follows him but becomes distracted by the cook dead in the corner.

She asks Ryan, 'What happened?'

'He attacked me when I came in,' Ryan responds. 'I had no choice.' Ryan continues to look around, but he cannot find anything they can wear. He then sees a door opening into a smaller room. He walks into the room, which appears to be a laundry room. He looks into the machines, and there he finds everything he needs in one go. He picks out a simple red dress for Ami and gives it to her. He also finds a jacket with a hoodie, which he puts on himself. They run to the entrance where Ryan first came in.

Ryan opens the door just slightly and looks outside. He hears the alarm still sounding, and lots of people are running around. It is complete chaos.

'Okay, keep your head down and follow me,' he tells Ami. 'If anything happens, then hide, understand?'

Ami agrees and Ryan throws open the door.

They quickly run through the masses in the direction of the tunnel Ryan came through when he came back from the supply run. They walk through the streets, and Ryan sees a guard standing on the corner with his machine gun. The guard look around, most likely to find Ryan and Ami. Ryan quickly drags Ami onto a side path, and they run along it. They head up into another street where their tent used to be. They run through the street and in the direction of the kitchen. As they run past the kitchen, Ryan can see a few women who recognise them, and they start to scream. Ryan and Ami quickly run until they get to Operations.

Of course, there are many guards in operation, and so Ryan and Ami walk into a side street again and walk around the guards and into the tunnel. They try to act normal, but of course Ryan and Ami are both terrified that someone will stop them. They find themselves at the entrance of the tunnel.

Beyond this point, there are no people walking, and so Ryan pulls out his gun and tells Ami they need to sprint to the side tunnel that leads outside. They start to run, but when they are almost at the side tunnel, Ryan sees two guards. 'Shit,' he says, but there is no time to look for another way out. 'Stay low,' says Ryan, and they start to run at the guards.

Whilst running, Ryan shoots his entire clip before they even see anyone coming. Ryan and Ami step over the bodies and crouch into the side tunnel. They quickly run through the tunnel, staying low, and eventually reach the metal frame. Ryan lifts the frame and tells Ami to hold it when she is outside.

Ami climbs through and holds the frame from the outside; she has trouble holding it because it is a very heavy metal frame.

Ryan quickly jumps outside the tunnel and, not even half a second later, Ami can no longer hold the frame and it slams shut with a loud noise. 'Oof that was close! Are you okay?' Ryan asks.

'Yes I'm fine. How is your shoulder?'

'It's okay, but we've got to keep moving. It's not safe here anymore.'

'I'm so glad you came back for me,' says Ami.

Ryan smiles and says, 'We are a team. We stick together.'

'What do we do now?'

'There's a town not far from here. I went there this morning. We were overrun by a few KBs, but I think right now it's safer to go there than stay here.

Maybe we can find some food and spend the night there, then tomorrow we will make a plan as to what we'll do next.'

Ryan and Ami start to jog in the direction of the village.

After journeying for a while, they arrive at the village border. They hide behind a fallen tree, and Ryan looks around to see if there are any KBs around, or even anyone from the resistance. Everything appears to be clear. It is late in the evening, and already it is getting dark; the birds can be heard singing in the trees.

Ryan and Ami take a moment of peace whilst they sit against the tree, enjoying the birdsong. But soon, Ryan stands up and tells Ami they should go in case anyone from the resistance comes looking for them. They slowly walk to one of the buildings on the border of where the village starts. They walk next to the building, sticking close to the walls, but after passing two buildings, Ryan hears something.

He tells Ami to stop moving, and silently he walks to the corner. He peeks around the corner, and there he sees a few KBs walking around. He quickly walks back to Ami and tells her that they need to find a different way. He looks around and there, across the street, he sees a passage leading to the backyards of houses. They quickly run across the street and into the passage, where they find a wooden fence to a backyard behind it.

Ryan looks around to see if there are any KBs. He then kicks the fence a few times, and two planks of wood fall loose. He crawls through and checks that everything is clear. He then signs to Ami to come through. They walk across the back yard and break down another fence to the second house; Ryan sees that the backdoor of the house is open.

'Maybe we will even find some food or water in the house,' says Ryan.

They walk to the house, and Ryan pulls out his gun. He slowly and silently enters the building, and checks every corner to make sure there is nobody in the house. He first walks into the kitchen to check for supplies, but everything is empty. 'Damn,' he mutters, and then walks into the living room. Ryan looks around the room; you can see there has not been anyone in this house for a very long time. All the furniture is very dusty, and there is a smell of neglect and emptiness.

Ryan walks over to the front door to look through the window to see if there is anyone on the street. He is about to look through the window when the door is kicked open from the outside, which hits Ryan against his head. He falls down; it takes him a few seconds to recover from the blow. He looks up, and there he sees a KB standing right in front of him.

The KB grabs Ryan's throat and throws him against the wall. He comes closer, ready to shoot Ryan. But then Ryan sees Ami picking up an old lamp, which she uses to hit the KB against the head. The KB falls down, and Ami continues to hit him; she is terrified but just wants to make sure it is dead. After a few more hits, Ryan stands up and quickly walks over to Ami.

'Ami, it's okay. I think he's dead.'

Ami hits the KB two more times and then drops the lamp and crawls away from the body. She is very upset, and so Ryan quickly walks over to her and comforts her.

'It's okay. It's okay. You saved my life. Thank you.'

Ryan helps Ami up, but then he hears the well-known ticking sound of KBs preparing to shoot their automatic rifles. 'Shit!' says Ryan, and quickly he pushes Ami behind the couch and dives behind it himself. Not long after, bullets rain through the room. The glass shatters, and Ryan and Ami are hit by debris from all sides. Ryan covers Ami to make sure she does not get hit, not knowing that he is probably more vulnerable than Ami. It takes several seconds for the shooting to stop, but it feels like so much longer—minutes.

Ryan looks up. He knows what will happen next, and pulls out his gun to reload it. He aims to the door and 3 KBs come rushing in, two through the door and one jumps through the shattered window.

Ryan shoots the two KBs near the door, and they go down fairly easy, but the KB that came through the window has reloaded his gun and starts shooting at Ryan. Ryan grabs Ami by her arm, and quickly they run outside and into the back yard.

They run to one of the fences, and Ryan jumps against it, causing the fence to break and fall over. They end up in an alley between two houses, and then make their way towards the main street.

Ryan gets some time to reload his gun again whilst they run to the main street.

They arrive at the corner, and Ryan looks around it to see if there are any KBs. He sees two KBs standing in the distance, but it looks like they are not looking his way.

'It's now or never,' says Ryan, and they start running along the buildings and in the direction of the forest. They arrive at the other side of the village, and Ryan looks back one last time before they journey in amongst the trees.

He sees one of the KBs that was behind them looking for them on the street. Ryan stops running, aims his gun and, in one shot, shoots down the KB. He then puts his gun away, and Ryan and Ami start to walk into the forest.

'It's getting dark. I think we should walk for just another hour, just to get away from this mess, and then we'll need to set up camp with the things we have.'

An hour passes, and you can see that Ryan is tired and worn out. They find a flat spot in the forest and throw down their stuff. Ryan sits down and looks in his backpack. He takes out two cans of food, which immediately cheers him up. He takes out his can-opener and opens the can, and begins eating like he has not eaten for days.

Ami sits next to him, staring in front of her. She is surprisingly quiet, but Ryan is too busy eating to notice. When he has finished, he then looks over to Ami and asks, 'Is everything ok?'

'Yes, fine, but what are we going to do now?' she says, sadness in her voice.

'It's very late, and I'm too tired to think of all that right now. Let's do it like this. We will sleep it off, and first thing tomorrow morning, we'll make a plan on what to do next.'

'Okay,' says Ami, and she smiles at Ryan.

Ryan smiles back and then removes his sleeping bag from his bag. He rolls it out and crawls into it, says goodnight, and falls asleep.

Ami is left sitting alone in the dark. She picks

up Ryan's jacket and lays it on the ground next to him. She lays down and makes herself comfortable, closes her eyes, and lets her mind go blank.

CHAPTER 6
WHAT TO DO NEXT

The following morning, Ryan and Ami wake to the sound of birds singing, with the sun shining through the trees and onto their faces. Ryan slowly stands up and stretches himself. Ami mimics Ryan by also stretching, and they both start to laugh.

Ryan stands up and walks around a bit, stretching his legs and enjoying the beautiful morning. He then sits down and takes out his last can of food. He grabs the can-opener, opens the can, and start eating.

Ami sits next to him and asks, 'So, what's the plan?'

Ryan looks up and says, 'I have been thinking about it and I think the best thing to do is find a safe place. My parents used to have a cabin in the woods, which would be perfect, but it is quite a distance away. But I do think it's our best bet. There is a city not far from here, and the cabin is on the other side of the city, deep in the forest.'

'That doesn't sound too hard. How long do you think it will take us to get there?'

'Well, first of all, we need supplies. The cabin is a few miles away from the city, so getting supplies will be harder. But I think, if everything goes well, then we should be able to get there in three or four days of walking.'

'So how are we going to get the supplies?' asks Ami.

'I think out best bet will be to look in the city. There are a lot of shops that still have supplies because, when the attacks happened, the city was the first place people left because there were so many KBs there. I don't know if they are still there, though…'

'It will be dangerous.'

'Yes,' Ryan agrees, 'but after that we will be safe from the outside world.'

Ryan stands up and reaches his hand out to

Ami. She takes his hands and helps her up. 'I'm sure there will be a road close by that we can follow to the city,' he states. 'I think it might be an idea if we just keep walking until it's dark.'

Ami smiles and says, 'I'm so glad we are friends.'

Ryan smiles back and starts to pack his bag.

The two start to walk through the forest. After walking for a good two hours, they still have not come across a road that leads to the city. Ryan tells Ami he will climb up one of the trees to see if he can see anything.

'Okay, but make sure you don't fall out of it again!' says Ami with a smile on her face.

Ryan looks around and sees a high tree, its branches sticking out, providing a perfect climbing frame. He throws down his backpack and starts to climb the tree. Once at the top, he looks around. He can see that they are surrounded by forest, but then, in the distance, he sees a road going up over one of the hills. He takes out his compass and sees that the road is north from where they are. He carefully climbs down and tells Ami it will not be long before they arrive at the road. 'Once we have found the road, it should lead us straight to the city,' Ryan tells her.

They start to walk in the direction of the road; it does not take long for them to arrive at a single-lane tarmac road, surrounded by forests on both sides.

'Cool, we've found it! Now all we have to do is follow the road in this direction,' Ryan says, pointing east.

They start to walk along the road for about an hour.

'I'm bored,' says Ami, and asks if they can make a pit stop soon.

'Yeah. I could use a break, too. We'll walk for another thirty minutes or so, and then we'll rest for a bit,' says Ryan.

They walk for another fifteen minutes, but then they stumble across a crashed car.

Ryan takes out his gun and tells Ami to stay back. He then slowly walks to the car and looks inside to see if anyone is in there. The car is empty, and so Ryan starts to walk around the car and looks at the forest on both sides of the road to make sure it's abandoned. It looks like the car has been left, and Ryan tells Ami that it is safe to come. 'I think it's a good place to rest for a while,' he says, and sits against the car.

It is a hot day, and Ryan is sweating a lot. He takes out his bottle of water and notices that it is almost empty. He takes a few sips until the bottle is empty, and says that they need to find some water soon.

Ami sits next to Ryan and takes a deep, sarcastic breath, 'I'm an AI and even I notice that it's really a hot day today,' she says.

Ryan laughs and tells her she is right. 'I think it's best if we take a break later today and then begin walking again once the sun is going down. We need to find some water and food soon, so keep an eye out if you see anything through the forest or along the road that we can use.'

Ryan and Ami sit against the car for another few minutes, enjoying the peace. After a while, Ryan takes a few breaths and stands up. He puts on his backpack and reaches his hand out to Ami to pull her up. They start to slowly walk along the road in the direction of the city. Ryan and Ami walk alongside the road for another hour; it is a very boring journey since there is nothing to do but follow the road.

Ryan soon becomes worn out because of the heat, and they decide to take a break for a few hours and then continue for another few hours until it gets dark. Ryan tells Ami that it's best if they take some rest under the shadows; they walk into the forest and there they find a nice tree, not too far away from the road, to sit under. Ryan throws down his stuff and makes himself comfortable against the tree. He takes a few deep breaths and then asks Ami how she is doing.

'I'm doing good. I hope we'll reach the city soon,' she says.

'Yeah, me too. I'll be glad when all of this is over and we can just enjoy a calm and relaxed life!'

'Yes. It's funny how things change. At one point I was just sitting in a small room, day in and day out, and now I'm walking in the outside world, having the adventure of a lifetime!'

Ryan smiles and says, 'Yeah, me too. Even though the world has turned to shit, at least I have made a new friend.'

'I thought we were more than friends?' Ami asks.

Ryan looks surprised and asks, 'What do you mean?'

'Well, we are partners aren't we? A team?'

Ryan smiles again. 'Yes, we are. The best team in the world.'

Ami smiles back and looks up at the sky. The light shines through the leaves of the trees; everything feels so peaceful.

Ryan looks at Ami and asks her if it was worth leaving the place she came from to live in a dangerous world. She looks at Ryan and says, 'I have been in that room all my life. My dad always told me that, one day, he would let me out and I could explore the world. But I guess this is not the way he meant it to be. But yes, I think it was worth it. I think life would not be worth living if you are forced just to stay in one place, all by yourself, for your entire life.'

Ryan looks down, a condescending look on his face, and tells Ami that he is happy he is not alone anymore. She sits closer to Ryan and lays her head on his shoulder. Ryan then rests his head against the back of the tree and, both with a small smile on their faces, they enjoy the peace and the sounds of nature.

Ryan soon falls asleep against the tree. A few hours later, Ami wakes him up and tells him that it is starting to cool down. He wakes up and notices that it is already late –evening. 'Thanks for waking me up,' he says. He tells Ami that they will walk for another few hours until the sun has set and, after that, they will set up camp in the forest for the night.

They start to walk back to the road and continue their journey.

Whilst walking, Ami asks if Ryan can tell her how the world looked before all this happened, and so Ryan begins to tell Ami that the world looked a lot more modern before everything went to hell.

'A year before the attack, the entire world was involved in a technology uprising. There were new things being invented every week to make our lives easier! I can still remember the first time they announced that you could buy bots to help you with your everyday tasks.' He smiled sadly. 'Everything went so fast. Within a year, almost every household had its own helper bot. We also had other really cool stuff, like virtual reality and holograms, that were all quite new. It was still a start but you could already play games with them or watch movies.'

'But with all this technology, there were also specific groups of people who did not like change, who did not trust it, and those people ended up attacking it. I'm sure they didn't mean for it to go so far, but it is what it is.'

Ami tells Ryan that the world sounds like it was a nice place before the attacks.

'Yeah, it was, but hey, see it like this. I would never have met you if all of this hadn't happened,' says Ryan.

Ryan and Ami continue walking alongside the road, talking about random things. After a few hours, Ryan notices that the sun has almost set, and he tells Ami that he thinks this is a good time to set up camp for the night. They walk a bit further, and they find a small forest path leading into the forest.

They follow the path and, not too far into the forest, they stumble across an abandoned campsite. There is an open space with an RV and a few tents around it. It looks like people lived there for quite some time, but now there is nobody to be seen.

Ryan and Ami slowly walk to the RV. Ryan takes out his gun and opens the door. He jumps inside but sees there is no one in it.

He walks outside again and says to Ami that he will check the tents to be sure. There are two tents open, and he can already see that there is nobody in either. He walks to the third tent, which is closed, and slowly opens the tent. When the tent opens just a little bit, a horrible smell hits Ryan in the face, and he has to fight the urge to throw up. He takes a quick look inside the tent and sees a decomposed body that has been left warming in the sun for the longest time.

He quickly closes the tent and tells Ami not to open it.

'Why? What's in it?' she asks, and Ryan tells her that there is someone in there that died a long time ago. Ami is still not completely used to being surrounded by death, and she takes a few steps back and avoids coming close.

'Can I look in the RV?' she asks.

'Sure,' Ryan says, and they both walk inside the VR. Ryan starts to check the cabins and, whilst doing that, he starts to laugh.

'Woohoo. It looks like we have some dinner tonight,' he says to Ami whilst holding two cans of chili.

Ami smiles and says, 'I wish I could eat. I wonder how those things taste.'

Ryan looks up and says, 'Consider yourself lucky. The taste is not worth going through the trouble of needing to keep finding food and water.' He then walks over to the back of the RV and there he finds a large twin bed. He feels the matrass, which is very soft. He then jumps on the bed and a bit of dust flies up.

'Wow, it's been a long time since I've lay on a bed!' he says, smiling.

Ami walks over to the bed and sits on it. For her, it is not that special since it does not really matter whether the surface she sits on is hard or soft, but she starts to bounce on the bed to share in Ryan's fun.

'Okay, I will go and make a fire so we can have a warm dinner tonight,' says Ryan, and he stands up and walks outside the RV. Ami stays inside the RV and has a look around; she is curious. She looks inside the drawers and closets. Ryan, meanwhile, walks into the denser forest and starts to pick out small branches that he can use to make a fire. It has been dry for weeks now, and so it does not take long for him to find some good branches he can use. He walks back to the campsite with the branches and lays them in a classic fireplace, surrounded by stones that the people who lived there before had made. He walks over to his backpack and takes out his lighter. He looks for some paper but he cannot find any in his bag.

He walks into the RV and there he sees Ami snooping around.

'Have you come across any paper?' he asks.

Ami walks over to one of the drawers and takes out some old newspapers, 'Here you go,' she says.

'Thanks,' says Ryan. He leaves the RV and

starts to make the fire.

From outside, he calls Ami and tells her that the fire is beginning to catch. Ami walks outside and sees Ryan taking some folding chairs from one of the tents.

He puts down the chairs, and they both sit in them. Ryan takes a can of food from his backpack and picks up a metal barbeque frame that is on the ground, and lays it over the fire. He opens up the can and puts it on the fire. He then asks Ami how she is doing.

'I'm doing fine. Why do you ask?' she responds.

'I was just wondering.'

'How are you doing?' she asks.

Ryan smiles and says that he is doing fine, too, but states that his arm still hurts, but it will be fine. Ryan looks at Ami. It is dark now, and through her dress, Ryan can see Ami's heart glowing light blue. It is a very relaxing thing to see.

Ryan takes the can of food from the fire and starts to eat it. He then looks up at the sky.

Ami also looks up and tells Ryan that the sky

Emiel Sleegers

looks pretty. Ryan agrees and tells her that it is getting late. 'I think I'm going to get some rest for tonight. Tomorrow we will wake up early to continue walking to the city. I would like you to stay in the RV tonight in case anything happens.'

Ami agrees and tells Ryan she will come soon. He stands up and walks into the RV.

He walks over to the bed and lets himself fall onto it. He closes his eyes and slowly starts to fall to sleep.

Not long after, Ami walks into the RV and closes the door. She looks around to see where she can lay down, and decides to rest next to Ryan. They both lay next to each other in the bed, with Ryan already in deep sleep. Ami also closes her eyes and asks her mind to switch off.

The following morning, Ryan wakes up early and, with sleepy eyes, looks around him and sees that Ami is not in the RV. He shocks himself awake and jumps up. He quickly walks to the door and opens

118

it. He looks around and sees Ami sitting in a folding chair reading what appears to be a comic book. Relief washes over him, and he walks over to Ami. He takes the seat next to her and says, 'Good morning. You scared me for a moment.'

Ami looks up and says, 'Good morning. What do you mean?'

'You weren't in the RV when I woke up and I thought something had happened.'

Ami smiles and tells Ryan she is sorry but she wanted to enjoy nature and she found a cool comic book.

'What kind of comic book is it?' he asks.

'I only read a few pages, but it is about a guy and a little girl that live in a world where a virus killed many people, and they both try to survive.'

'How ironic. Add some KBs and it's just like our life!' Ryan takes his backpack and looks inside. 'Damn it,' he says in a soft voice.

Ami looks up and asks what's wrong.

'It looks like I won't be having any breakfast today,' he says, disappointment on his face. 'Oh well. I think it'd be best if we start walking again soon. It feels like it's going to be a warm day today and it's still a bit cool right now.'

Ami agrees, and Ryan starts to pack his bag. He walks into the RV and takes some things he can use in the future, such as cups and forks and knives. He then walks outside and sees Ami waiting for him, all ready to go.

They start to walk back in the direction of the road. 'I'm going to miss that bed,' Ryan muses. 'It's been a long time since I slept that well!'

Ami smiles and, with a funny but sarcastic voice, says, 'Yeah, me too.'

They both start to laugh for a moment, and then all falls quiet again.

After a few minutes, they arrive at the road again and continue their walk in the direction of the city. After walking for a while, Ami hears a sound in the distance. She asks Ryan what it is, and they stop walking for a moment. Ryan listens closely; he hears what sounds like a lot of people walking. The sound comes closer and closer, and Ryan and Ami decide that hiding out behind some trees next to the road is the best choice.

Not long after they sit behind the trees, Ryan peeks over and sees a mass of KBs walking towards them from the distance. With a frightened look, he signals to Ami to be very quiet and not to show herself. Ryan stays behind the trees and does not peek around them anymore because he does not want to risk being seen.

He hears the KBs coming closer and closer; his heart starts pounding in his chest. He waits to see what happens. Luckily, he hears that the KBs did not see them and that they walk past Ryan and Ami. After a while, Ryan peeks out again and sees the KBs walking off into the distance, far away from them.

He takes a deep breath and crawls over to Ami. 'Okay, I think it's safe. I don't know where they were going but I'm lucky we are not in that place!'

Both flooded with relief, they slowly stand up and come out of cover. Ryan checks both sides of the street to make sure there are no KBs nearby. When it looks like it's safe, Ryan and Ami start to walk again.

After a few hours, the sun is high in the sky, and Ryan starts to get really warm. 'I think it's time for a pit stop soon,' he says to Ami.

They reach a hill where the road continues to pave. The hill is pretty steep, and Ryan and Ami start to walk up it. They arrive at the top; from there, they can look out over the forest. They see a beautiful skyline with the city in the background; the sun shines between the buildings.

Ryan and Ami take a moment to look at the view and, while doing so, Ami says that it looks amazing.

Ryan replies, 'Yes, it sure does,' and he takes a deep breath of fresh air. 'Okay, I have been in the city many times before. Do you see that big skyscraper over there? That's where the shopping centre is. That's where we need to go,' says Ryan, pointing his finger to a tall building that reaches high above the other buildings.

Ami smiles and, with an excited voice, says, 'I would love to get some new cloths when we are there.'

Ryan laughs and tells Ami that, when they are there, they will do some clothes shopping.

Ryan and Ami start to walk downhill. It is a lot

easier for them, and sometimes they even walk too fast and need to slow down. It does not take long for them to get down the hill, and when there, they walk up to a big tree next to the road and sit under it, deep in the shadows, and take a break.

Ryan starts to complain that he is hungry. 'We need to find some food and water soon. With this heat I'm starting to run out of energy. Soon I'll be dehydrated,' he says.

Ami tells Ryan that she is sure they will find something soon.

They both lean back against the tree, and Ryan closes his eyes for a moment and takes some rest.

Ami, on the other hand, looks up through the trees to where the sun is shining through the leaves and just enjoys the view.

CHAPTER 7

A JOURNEY TO THE CITY

Half an hour has passed and Ryan and Ami decide to move on again. Ryan stands up and stretches himself. He then pulls Ami up, and together they start to walk in the direction of the city.

Ryan is starting to get dehydrated by now, and he is getting worried that he will not be able to walk for much longer. Nonetheless, they keep walking for another fifteen minutes and then, in the distance, Ryan sees what looks like a building on the side of the road. When they get closer, Ryan sees that it is a restaurant.

Immediately, Ryan cheers up and starts to walk a bit faster. 'There must be some water and food there,' he says, excitement in his voice.

Ami also gets excited because Ryan is happier.

They both start to jog to the restaurant.

When they arrive, Ryan tries to open the door but finds it is locked. Luckily, the door is made from glass, and so Ryan looks around, picks up a big stone from a few feet away, tells Ami to step back, and then throws the stone straight through the glass.

The glass shatters and makes a large hole big enough for Ryan to step through. He goes into the restaurant and tells Ami to be careful. He then immediately walks over to the kitchen; it has not been used for a long time because everything is greasy and dusty. But, of course, Ryan does not mind that. He starts to check all the cabinets. There, he finds a whole bunch of cans of food. He grabs all he can carry and puts them in his backpack. He looks around and sees a fridge, where he finds one last six-pack of bottled water. He pulls off the plastic and opens up one of the bottles. It takes Ryan only a few seconds to drink down the entire bottle and, with a relieved expression on his face, he starts to put the rest of the bottles in his backpack. By now, his backpack is starting to get really heavy, and he is having trouble lifting it.

When he is getting ready to leave, Ami comes running into the kitchen with a frightened look on her face. 'I heard some people outside!' she says.

Ryan's joy immediately fades away, and he lays his backpack in the corner and pulls out his gun. He tells Ami to stay in the kitchen and then slowly crouches down and overs over to the other room. There, he sees two men coming to the door. Ryan quickly hides behind the bar.

The men climb through the door and then turn around to look outside.

When they turn around, Ryan jumps out from behind the bar and tells the men to put their hands up.

The men quickly turn around and, as a reaction, go to grab their guns.

'I wouldn't do that if I were you,' Ryan warns.

The men slowly move their hands away from the guns and put their hands up. Ryan tells them to drop their weapons and backpacks. When the men are about to drop their backpacks, they stop and start to smile. Ryan thinks it's strange, and asks them if they think this is funny. But not long after saying that, he sees that there is a man standing right behind Ryan, a gun aimed at his head.

Ryan drops his gun. 'What do you want?' he asks.

'Revenge,' says one of the guys. Ryan then realises that they are probably from the resistance.

Behind him, he hears the click of a gun, and sees that the guy is about to shoot him. Ryan sees no way out, and so he closes his eyes and waits for the shot.

A few seconds later, all he hears is the man making a strange sound, like he is gasping for air.

'What's wrong?' asks one of the men, but soon after asking, the guy falls to the ground. A knife is planted firmly in his back. Ami stands behind him, a look of fear on her face.

The two men standing in front of Ryan grab their guns, and Ryan quickly grabs Ami and they both dive behind the bar. In the process, Ryan manages to grab his gun from the ground, and he prepares himself to shoot.

The men split up and start shooting in the direction of Ryan. Ryan waits for a few seconds until he hears that one of the men is very close to him. He looks around the corner and sees that one of the men is reloading his weapon. Ryan aims his gun and shoots the man three times in his chest.

The guy drops his gun and falls down to the ground. Ryan then tries to look around to see where the other guy is; he notices he is trying to flank him.

Ryan crawls around the corner of the bar and makes sure the other guy does not see him. He then walks alongside the bar and is now standing only a few feet away from the guy.

Ryan jumps out and shoots the guy in the back.

The guy falls to the ground and it gets quiet for a moment.

Ryan is still not sure what just happened and he looks at the men he just shot, He then realizes that Ami is still behind the bar and he runs to her. He looks behind the bar and sees Ami sitting against it, her arms covering her face. He walks over to Ami and wants to touch her arm, but Ami is frightened and pulls her arms tightly around herself. Ryan quickly grabs both of her arms and holds her in controlled way whilst saying, 'It's me, Ami.'

Ami then looks up and sees that Ryan is sitting right in front of her.

'Is it over?' she asks in a scared voice.

'Yes, it's over,' Ryan reassures her.

Ami gives Ryan a long hug and tells him that she was really scared that something would happen to him. He comforts Ami and then stands up and walks over to the dead guy with the knife in his back. Ryan takes out the dead man's gun, removes the ammunition, and puts it into his own gun. He then walks over to the other guy. Ryan opens up the man's backpack and finds some more ammunition, a bottle of water, and some basic survival supplies. He takes the backpack with him, and then walks over to Ami who, by now, has calmed down. He tells her that it's best for them to get far away from this place because it isn't safe.

They walk outside of the restaurant and there Ryan sees a rusty pickup truck; it looks like it belonged to the resistance guys. Ryan walks over to the truck and sees that the keys are still in the car. He smiles and tells Ami this will help them to get to the city a whole lot faster. He throws his backpack into the back of the car and tells Ami to get into the passenger seat. Ryan sits in the driver's seat and starts the car. He sees that there is probably just enough fuel to get to the city. He drives off the parking lot and onto the road, heading in the direction of the city.

After driving for a while, Ryan sees it is getting dark; he also feels a bit worn out by everything that has happened during the course of the day.

The city is still a few hours' drive away, and so Ryan decides to overnight one last time before arriving at the city. 'I think it's a good idea if we get some sleep now. Tomorrow we will arrive in the city,' Ryan says to Ami.

Ami agrees, and Ryan drives up into a small forest path and drives the car into the bushes so that no one can see it.

Ryan and Ami step out of the car and walk into the forest. There, they find a tree that has fallen and split in two, and they sit on it. Ryan notices that he has forgotten his backpack, and so he walks back to the car, grabs his back and also the one he took from the dead resistance guy, and walks back to Ami. He sits down next to Ami and hands her the backpack. 'Here. In case you ever want to easily carry something with you and to keep your stuff safe,' says Ryan.

Ami smiles and says, 'Thanks! You're always are so good to me, Ryan. You always protect me so well. I want to be able to protect you, too. Maybe you can teach me how to shoot a gun in case we ever get into a situation again like at the restaurant?'

Ryan agrees and tells Ami he will give her a crash course in the morning. He finishes his food and tells Ami that it is getting late. 'I'm going to get some sleep,' he tells her.

Ami agrees, and they both walk to the car. Ryan steps into the driver's seat and makes himself comfortable. Ami also gets into the car and sits in the passenger seat.

They both close their eyes and fall asleep.

The following morning, the sun is shining through the windshield, and Ryan wakes up. He yawns and looks over to Ami, who is looking around the dashboard. 'Good morning,' he says, and Ami looks over at Ryan and smiles.

'Hey, how did you sleep?' asks Ami.

'I've had better, but I got a few good hours in. Today will be a busy day, so let's get some food, learn some basic defence techniques, and then we'll go off to the city!'

Ami reacts with happiness and excitement, and they both step out of the car.

Ryan walks over to his backpack and takes out another can of food. He opens it up and starts eating. Ami sits next to him and asks if it is hard to learn how to shoot.

'Nah, it's not very hard. It just takes some practice to become better at it,' he tells her.

'So what do you expect to find in the city today?' Ami asks.

'Well, the plan is to get a lot of supplies from the shopping centre, and now we have a car we will be able to get enough supplies to stay away from the city for a long time. When all this started, the first thing that got overrun were the cities, and so we do need to be very careful. I hope we won't come across any other KBs.'

Ami looks a bit worried whilst Ryan is telling her all this.

'Don't worry. We will stick together and, after today, you also will be able to defend yourself a lot better,' says Ryan with a kind smile on his face.

Ryan finishes his food and tells Ami that, if she wants, he can teach her how to shoot right now. Ami says yes with excitement in her voice. He stands up and grabs a few empty cans. He also grabs his gun, and they both walk a bit further into the forest.

Ryan walks over to a tree that has fallen over and places the cans on the trunk. He then walks back to Ami and takes out his gun. 'Okay, so it is very simple. What you want to do, when you want to shoot, you need to flip this switch—this is the safety switch—and you then want to hold your arms straight and aim at the target you want to hit. When you feel confident that you are going to hit your target, you want to press the trigger.' He points at the various parts of the gun as he speaks. 'Now, this gun does not give a lot of knockback, but do be aware that there will be some knockback as soon as you shoot. One last thing: a gun is not a toy. You've seen that over the past few days, so when you shoot, make sure you mean it. Also, ammunition is scarce, so if you have to shoot, make every shot count, okay?'

Ami agrees with everything. Ryan shoots one of the cans to show Ami how to do it. He walks over to the can and puts it back on the tree. He then walks back to Ami and hands her the gun.

'Okay. Now, aim the gun at one of the cans,' Ryan says, and Ami starts to aim. Ryan moves her arm a bit higher and says, 'Okay. Now take off the safety and, when you are ready, press the trigger.'

Ami takes off the safety and takes a few seconds to aim. She then fires the gun, which gives more knockback then she expected. She looks a bit scared because of the shock, and unfortunately misses her target.

'It's okay,' says Ryan. 'Try again. Take all the time you need.'

Ami aims her gun again and fires again. This

time, she prepares herself for the knockback and hits her target.

Ryan looks surprised but, then again, he did expect that it would be different to when teaching a human to shoot!

Ami then focuses her attention on the other cans and shoots all of them off the trunk in her first try. She starts to laugh and gets all excited because she hit all the cans.

'Wow, amazing job!' says Ryan.

Ami thanks Ryan and says, 'That was fun!' and hands the gun back to Ryan.

'Yeah it was. But remember that, out there, when you aim your gun at someone else, make sure you mean it—and you can deal with the consequences. Emotionally.'

Ami nods and tells Ryan that, from now on, she will do everything she can to protect him. He thanks her and smiles, and they both head back to the car.

Ryan puts the gun in his backpack and then takes out another pistol that he took from one of the resistance fighters. He gives it to Ami and tells her to put it in her backpack. 'Now, let's do this,' he says, and throws his backpack in the car. Ami also lays her backpack carefully in the car and gets into the passenger seat.

Ryan takes off the branches that cover the back of the car and gets in. He starts the engine and reverses backwards before driving out of the forest. Soon they are on the main road once again, and begin driving in the direction of the city.

CHAPTER 8
THE CITY

They drive towards the city, and already they can see the skyline. The sun is hanging low, and it is a beautiful sight. They drive for only a few more hours, and soon then arrive at the city border.

Ryan and Ami drive over one of the main roads and, when they get closer to the city blocks, they see that there are KBs hanging around, watching the streets. Ryan had expected this and, luckily, there are not as many as he thought there would be—at least, not as far as he can see.

He stops the car and looks around him.

'So what are we going to do now?' asks Ami

'Wait, I have an idea,' says Ryan, and he starts to drive down a quiet street within the distance of a small train station. He drives the car on to the tracks

137

and starts to follow them.

Ami and Ryan start to laugh as the car bumps over the tracks. Ryan keeps looking out of the window to make sure that he is still going in the right direction. There is a large skyscraper he can look at to pinpoint where the shopping centre is located.

After a while, they are only a few blocks away from the shopping centre, and they will not be able to drive any further without being noticed. Ryan parks the car next to the train tracks in-between some construction equipment to make sure no one sees the car. They both get out of the car and grab their backpacks.

'We will need to walk from here,' says Ryan, and he pulls out a map that Ami found in the car dashboard. He places the map on the hood of the car and shows Ami where they need to walk.

They are approximately four blocks away from the shopping centre, but there are a number of alleyways in the city that they can use to move around without being noticed by any KBs.

'Okay, when we start to move, I need you to

stay very close to me,' instructs Ryan.

Ami agrees, and they prepare to walk over to the shopping centre.

'I would like you to keep your gun out at all time, just in case,' says Ryan.

Ami takes the gun from her backpack and they start to walk towards a back alley that leads into the resident areas of the city. They find themselves at a fence, and Ryan helps Ami to climb over it. He then throws his backpack over, and takes a run and jump. With some effort, he climbs over the fence and then picks up his backpack again. They start to walk towards the alley and around the corner—and that is when they see two KBs standing at the end of the alley, leading into the street.

Ryan quickly drags Ami behind a trash container and tells her to get her gun ready. 'Okay, this is the plan: you aim your gun at the left KB. I will count to three and then you will shoot. I will do the same for the KB on the right.'

Ami starts to aim her gun at the left KB and Ryan does the same for the right KB.

He starts to count. 'Three, two, one... Shoot!'

he says, and they both fire two rounds into the KBs. The KBs go down nice and easy, and Ryan tells Ami to stay behind the container until he calls her. He silently walks to the downed KBs and looks around the corner and into the street to make sure no other KBs have noticed them.

In the city, it's common to hear shooting in the distance, but most of the time it will be the KBs that are shooting. Luckily, because of this, the KBs don't come to investigate every single shot they hear.

Ryan calls Ami over, and she quickly runs to meet him. He looks around the street and sees that there are some more KBs standing in the distance on the left-hand side of the street. Luckily, the shopping centre is to the right side, and Ryan and Ami walk through the streets and away from the KBs, pressing themselves against the alley walls to keep from being seen.

After walking for about a hundred feet, Ryan sees a store across the street with the door wide open. He looks around again to make sure there are no KBs nearby, and then he tells Ami they are going to make a run for it. 'Okay. Let's go!' whispers Ryan, and they both run across the street and into the store.

The store appears to be a hardware store, so unfortunately they do not find any supplies there. But Ryan spots a nice crowbar that might come in handy later on, which he takes and straps to the side of his backpack. They then both walk to the back of the store, where Ryan tries to open a wooden door that leads into another room.

The door is locked, but Ryan already has a smile on his face because he has the crowbar. 'How ironic,' he murmurs as he sticks the crowbar in-between the door. He gives it a few hard pulls and the door breaks open. They find themselves in a storage room, where they see several boxes and cabins. A desk sits in the middle of the room. Ryan walks over to the desk and opens the top drawer, and sure enough finds a handful of bullets he can use for his own gun. He gives Ami a few bullets and tells her to reload her gun. Ryan does the same with his gun. He looks around and sees a metal door on the right-hand side of the room at the back. They walk over to the door and Ryan opens it; it is unlocked, and they find themselves in another alleyway, one block from where they started.

They walk through the alleyway and Ryan sees that they cannot walk into the street from the right side because there is debris from a fallen building blocking the road.

'Maybe we can go the other way?' says Ami.

'Yes, good idea,' says Ryan, and they start to walk in the other direction.

There is a corner that leads onto the street, but Ryan sees that there are three KBs standing right in front of the exit. He tells Ami to stay back, and he also takes a few steps back himself. But then comes the sound of breaking glass, and the two realise Ryan knocked over some glass wine bottles.

'Shit!' Ryan exclaims, and already they can hear the KBs walking towards them.

Ryan and Ami quickly run back, and Ryan tells Ami to prepare to shoot. They both hide behind a few small bins, and then they see the KBs coming around the corner. The KBs start to shoot at them, and Ryan and Ami starts shooting back. As they shoot, Ryan sees Ami is too scared because the bullets are passing by close to her.

'Ami, I need you now!' screams Ryan, and he continues shooting. 'Stay focused. Do it for me!' He shoots down two of the KBs before his ammo runs out. He tries to reload the gun, but there is no time—the KBs are coming too close.

The KB comes closer and almost hits Ryan.

The KB is now so close he can easily hit Ryan, but right at that moment he wants to make the killing shot, Ami shoots the KB.

Ryan takes a deep breath of relief and thanks Ami. He looks over and sees that Ami is terrified of the firefight. He moves over to her and sits next to her; he wants to comfort her but, before he can say anything, Ami falls into his arms and hugs onto him tightly.

'It's okay, it's okay. You did good,' says Ryan.

'I'm so sorry I couldn't help you…'

'You saved my life, Ami,' he smiles. 'You're beginning to save me more than I do you! Trust me, after a while, you'll get used to this stuff, believe me.' Ryan helps Ami up and reloads his gun. He asks Ami how many bullets she has left, and she tells him she has just nine left.

'It looks like we are running low on ammo. Make sure to shoot only when you have to from now on,' Ryan advises her.

They start to walk towards the street and, only a few feet away from the street, a KB turns around the corner and sees Ryan and Ami. Ryan pulls out his gun but, before he can shoot, he hears a shot and the KB falls down—Ami beat him to it and manages to shoot the KB first.

Ryan starts to laugh and says, 'Thanks again!'

They walks down the street and look around the corner to make sure there are no more KBs hanging around. Ryan sees a lot of KBs standing on the street corners and hanging around what appears to be an old police station. Unfortunately, all the KBs are standing in the street Ryan and Ami need to walk through to get to the shopping centre.

Ryan turns his head around and tells Ami to stay close. They then both walk very slowly through the street, sticking against the walls. It seems like the KBs do not notice that they are there because none of them look in their direction.

Ryan sees an open door not far from him; it leads into an apartment building. They are only ten feet away from the building, but then Ryan feels someone grabbing his shoulder and a gun pressed against his head. Ami also gets grabbed, and she tries to scream but someone holds a hand over her mouth.

'Be quiet and do what we say,' says a deep voice.

Ryan and Ami then are pushed in the direction of the open apartment building. They get pushed into the building and made to walk through a hallway. They enter the first apartment and get thrown to the ground. Ryan sees a man he does not recognise closing the curtains in front of the window so that the KBs cannot see them. He then starts to look around and sees two men standing in front of him. They look like resistance guys, but Ryan does not recognise either of them.

'You really aren't easy to kill!'

Ryan recognises the voice, and then sees the boss of the resistance walking in front of him. He is confused; he does not understand why the resistance want him dead so bad that even the boss leaves everything to find him.

'What are you doing here?' Ryan asks, his tone angry.

The boss smiles evilly, and then hits Ryan against the head with the side of his gun.

'Leave him alone!' screams Ami.

Ryan gets back up, and the boss now places his gun against the front of Ryan's head.

'So you are going to tell me everything I want to know about your little girlfriend?' asks the boss as he looks at Ami.

'What? Why do you care?' Ryan asks.

'I just want to know where we stand. I want to know what she is and why she is so special.'

Ryan says nothing and gets hit in the head again. 'Okay, okay,' says Ryan. 'What do you want to know?'

'Well, let's start with why you keep her hanging around you. She's a damn KB!'

'She isn't a KB!' says Ryan with determination.

'Then what is she?'

'She's my friend! And friends stick together.'

The boss gives a sarcastic laugh and says, 'You make me sick. How can you be friends with something that kills your own race?'

'She isn't one of them! She's way more than just a simple KB. She's above them! She's one of us!'

The boss gets angry and hits him again. Ami wants to get closer to Ryan, but she gets held back by one of the men.

Ryan spits blood to the ground and says, 'What are you doing here anyway? Don't you have your resistance to lead?'

With an angry voice the boss replies, 'There is no resistance anymore! Right after you left we got overrun by an army of KBs! You don't happen to know anything about that, do you?'

'What? Why would I know?' Ryan asks.

'Well, maybe your little girlfriend knowns. After all, she *is* an AI,' he says sarcastically.

Ryan looks at Ami and says, 'She would never do that. For the last time, she has nothing to do with KBs!'

'Nah, I think she does. I think that they developed a KB that looks like a human and acts like a human to spy on us.'

Ryan laughs and says, 'Do you even hear yourself? Why would the KBs go to the effort of making a better version of themselves to wipe out the very few people that are left on this god-forsaken Earth?!'

Ami looks frightened and does not understand what's going on. 'I didn't do anything!' she screams, and immediately one of the men puts a hand over her mouth.

'Leave her alone!' yells Ryan.

'Well, it doesn't matter now anyway. Your journey will end here,' says the boss. He then points his gun at Ryan's head and pulls back the hammer of the gun.

Ami tries to get lose in the hope she can jump in front of Ryan, but with no luck.

Ryan continues to look angry and determined, and at the moment the boss wants to shoot Ryan, he makes one last try and jumps up against the man. The boss loses his balance and falls to the ground, shooting once, with the bullet rushing into the wall next to Ryan. The man then jumps up and grabs his gun. With an outraged look on his face, he is about to shoot Ryan until he suddenly is distracted by a sound.

Ryan starts to smile because he knows the sound all too well. It's the sound of KBs warming up their guns.

Ryan screams at Ami to stay low, and Ryan crawls behind the couch. Just a few seconds after, the room is filled with flying bullets. Everything shatters around them, and Ryan ties to look around to see if Ami is okay. He sees that a few of the resistance guys, including the one who had been holding Ami, have been shot. Ami appears to be fine, and is taking cover behind a thick leather chair, her hands covering her face. She stays low as the bullets fly through the top of the chair.

After a short while, the shooting stops, and Ryan quickly jumps up, runs to Ami, and grabs her by her arms. They both run through the back of the house and out into the kitchen. The kitchen door leads to the back but it is locked. Luckily, however, the door is made of glass; Ryan grabs a chair and throws it straight through the door.

He lets Ami climb through first, and then he climbs through himself. They end up in the alley, and look around them, looking for the best way to get to safety. There is an exit to the street not far from them, but then Ryan hears someone walking. He and Ami quickly dive behind one of the big metal trash containers and wait.

A KB comes around the corner, apparently to investigate the noise of the window breaking. Ryan grabs a metal pipe out of a pile of debris just behind them and waits for the KB to come closer. He then jumps out in front of the KB, which then tries to shoot him, but Ryan pushes his gun to the side. The KB fires one shot into the floor next to Ryan, but Ryan bashes his head in with the pipe. He continues to hit the KB until he can no longer move. The head of the KB is completely crushed.

Ryan is out of breath and takes a moment to recover. He then tells Ami it's safe and that she can come out. When Ami comes out, they can hear the KBs started to fire again inside the house; it's an overwhelmingly loud sound.

Ryan and Ami run to the corner of the street,

and Ryan peeks around it to see if there are any KBs looking for them. He sees around five or six, all lined up in front of the house, shooting at it. Their guns glow red from the heat of the bullets.

Ryan turns his head to Ami and says 'Okay, screw the food. We need to get out of here. I think our best bet is to pick the alley next to the skyscraper. There seem to be no KBs there.'

Ryan grabs Ami's hand and they run across the street toward the skyscraper.

Halfway down the street, two KBs that are shooting at the house notice Ami and Ryan escaping, and they start to shoot at them. Ryan and Ami quickly take cover behind a car. Ryan wants to grab his gun but notices it's missing. Ami sees this, and quickly removes her backpack, takes out her gun and gives it to Ryan. The KBs start to come closer and are constantly shooting at the two of them. Ryan tries to shoot the KBs, but it is difficult because a shower of bullets scatters from all sides.

Ryan yells to Ami over the sound of the bullets hitting next to them. 'They are getting too close! Our only chance is to make a sprint for the alley.'

Ryan waits for the KBs to reload; they are now standing only a few feet away from Ryan and Ami. But just in time, their guns need to reload. Ryan and Ami jump up and run towards the alley. As they run, Ryan manages to shoot one of the KBs, but by now more KBs have noticed them and they start to shoot.

The bullets fly around them, but Ryan and Ami are close to the alley. They run around the corner and there they are met by two KBs waiting for them.

'Shit!' screams Ryan, and he grabs Ami by her arm. They run back onto the street and hide behind one of the big concrete flowerpots positioned in front of the skyscraper. Ryan and Ami are being trapped in from all sides now, and they decide to make a run for the skyscraper entrance—it's their only chance.

They run towards the doors, and Ryan shoots a few bullets into the glass so that it breaks. They jump through the glass and roll into the lobby. Ryan looks behind him; the KBs are getting closer.

'There!' he says, pointing at the stairway. 'I saw a sign saying there is a parking lot in this building.

Maybe we can cut through there!'

They run to the stairway door and Ryan kicks it open. They find themselves in a metal stairway that goes up and down. They run down, but after running down just one stair they are met with a metal door leading to the parking lot; it is locked up with a big chain.

Ryan looks at the lock and tries to shoot it, but with no luck; the lock is just too strong and Ryan knows it. 'There's no way we can get through this,' he says.

Ryan and Ami run back upstairs and want to go back into the lobby, but the KBs are already inside the building. They see Ryan and Ami, and start to shoot.

They are pushed back into the stairway, and are faced with only one option: go up.

They run upstairs and can hear the KBs filtering into the stairway. After running up a few floors, they come across a dead soldier; he has been dead for a while and it's not a pretty sight. Ryan sees an assault rifle lying next to him, and so he grabs it. The soldier also has a magazine in his front pocket, but it is covered with decomposed flesh. Ryan slowly picks out the magazine whilst holding back the urge to throw up. They then continue to run upstairs.

They have no time to think about what to do; right now, they have to find a way to get out of the building.

Most of the doors into the stairway are locked; it seems like a big part of the building went into lockdown a long time ago.

They arrive at the thirteenth floor, and there Ryan tries to push open the door. The door opens, and Ryan and Ami run inside. Ryan looks around and sees a cabinet standing close to the door. 'Here, help me with this,' he says to Ami. They push the cabinet against the door. They then start walking through the room to see if there is a way out.

They walk all the way to the back of the room. The outer walls are made of glass, and you can look all over the city. It looks like there is no way out, and then they hear that the KBs are breaking through the door.

'What do we do now?' asks Ami, clearly terrified.

'There is only one thing we can do. Fight,' says Ryan. He pushes over a table to allow them to take cover behind it. 'I need your help for this, Ami. Take cover and prepare to shoot whatever comes through that door.'

The tension is high, and even though Ami is really scared, she pulls herself together and they both aim their weapons at the door. They know they do not have a lot more bullets, and Ryan says to Ami with a soft voice, 'Make every shot count.'

Not long after, the KBs push away the cabin behind the door and the door flies open.

Ami takes the first shot and shoots the first KB down with one well-placed fire. Then three more KBs come through the door, and Ryan and Ami both start to shoot. The KBs shoot back at Ryan, and he is forced to take cover. Ami sees this and quickly shoots the KB who aims at Ryan. The KB goes down in two shots; the other KBs focuses their attention on Ami, and Ami all too quickly gets shot in the arm. She takes cover behind the table, and Ryan screams out to ask if she is okay.

'Yes, I'm fine,' she says.

Ryan gets angry and empties his magazine on the remaining two KBs. It does not take long for them to go down, and then all falls quiet. Ryan shuffles over to Ami and asks her if she is alright. He looks at her arm and sees that the wound is closing itself up. They both take a deep breath and spend a moment immersed in peace. Then Ryan says, 'This is our change,' and he stands up and reaches his hand out to Ami. He helps her up and they slowly, but with caution, walk to the door.

'I'm out of ammo. How much do you have left?' Ryan asks her.

Ami checks her gun and says, 'I have three bullets left.' She gives Ryan the gun because she thinks he has more use for it. They walk over to the door and when, they are about to walk outside, they hear a click.

Ryan feels a hot-and-cold sensation across his body, and then he hears someone say, 'Drop your god damn weapon!'

Ryan knows the voice all too well by now, and he and Ami slowly turn around. He sees the resistance boos standing at the back of the room, his back to the big windows. There is a bright light shining through the windows, and Ryan cannot see everything clearly, but it appears that the boss has been shot. His arm seeps blood, and he is full of scratches and small wounds.

Ryan slowly throws his gun on the ground and, in an angry voice, asks, 'What do you want now?'

The boss gives an evil smile and says, 'Nothing.' He then aims his gun and is about to shoot Ryan.

'Look out!' screams Ami, and she jumps in front of Ryan. The shot sounds, and Ami falls to the ground. She has been shot in her chest. Ryan rolls over and grabs the gun. He then shoots the boss in the chest. With tears in his eyes, he walks forward to the boss, who now is slowly collapsing, and shoots him once again in the chest. He keeps walking and then shoots the boss one final time in the head. The man falls backwards and through the window.

Ryan walks over to the window and looks down to take one last glimpse of the boss falling all the way down.

Then it strikes him what just happened. He

turns around and sees Ami lay on the ground. She is not moving. With tears in his eyes, he runs over to her and rolls her over. Ami has been shot in her heart, and is slowly shutting down.

'No, no, no, no! Please tell me you're okay,' says Ryan.

In Ami's final moments, she lays her hand on Ryan's cheek and, with a soft voice, says, 'Thank you for protecting me.'

Ryan starts to cry and keep saying, 'It can't end like this!' He cries and repeats the words over and over again.

Ami smiles as she looks into Ryan's eyes, and then she closes her eyes and her hand falls down.

Ryan sits in the middle of the room with Ami in his arms and tears in his eyes. He cannot believe what just happened and he does not know what to do. He looks down at Ami and tells her he is sorry. He then gives her a soft kiss on the forehead and hugs her tightly.

TWO MONTHS LATER

Ryan is sitting in front of a nice, quiet lake with a cabin behind him.

Everything is peaceful, the sun is hanging low, and the birds can be heard singing.

He hears something and looks behind him. He watches as Ami walks to him with a glass of lemonade in her hands. She sits down next to him and hands him the glass. She then holds his arm and lays her head on his shoulder.

They both smile, and Ryan stares across the lake.

He remembers all too clearly what happened in the city…

Ryan is sitting on the ground with Ami's lifeless body in his hands. He is crying. Then he says to himself, 'No! This is not the end! I refuse to let this be the end!'

He lifts Ami up and walks out of the door and into the stairway. Carefully, he walks down the stairs and arrives at the ground floor. He opens the door slightly and looks around him to see if there are any KBs close by.

There is no one; it is almost as if time has stood still. There is no shooting and no loud sounds. The only thing he can hear is his own heart, knocking loudly against his ribcage.

He walks out of the skyscraper and there, not far from the entrance, he sees the resistance boss lay on the ground in a big pool of blood. It is not a pretty sight. Ryan looks away and walks past him. He begins to run through the streets and alleys towards where he left the car. With tears in his eyes, and heavily out of breath, he arrives at the car and, to his relief, finds everything is still how he left it.

He carefully places Ami into the back of the car and gets in the driver's seat. He starts the car and begins to drive on the highway, away from the city. He drives as fast as he can until he arrives at the road he and Ami walked down when they were on their way to the city. He drives in the direction of the village and through the streets. He sees the streets scattered with bodies—both KBs and humans.

It's like there had been a war going on.

Ryan keeps driving, but soon turns left onto another tarmac road. After driving for about an hour, he arrives at the forest border. He drives through the forest as long as he can until the car gets stuck in between the trees. He then gets out and lifts Ami out of the truck. He walk through the forest with Ami in his arms.

Ami is beginning to feel heavy, but Ryan ignores the pain and keeps on going without taking a break.

He arrives at a hillside and walks along it. Then he sees the door of the house. The place he first met her. He kicks open the door and runs through the living room and into the hallway. He starts to cry again, but he pulls himself together and runs into one of the rooms. He throws everything from one of the metal tables and carefully lays Ami onto its surface.

'Okay, everything will be alright. I can do this,' he says to himself.

He looks at Ami and strokes her hair. He then runs into one of the other rooms where there are old prototypes that look like Ami. He grabs one of the bodies that looks most like Ami and lays it on the ground. He then feels her chest and tries to find a way to open it; apparently, the chest plate can be opened by pushing against it in an upwards motion.

Ryan is now looking at the heart of the AI. He carefully unplugs the wires; there is some liquid leaking from the heart, but the wires themselves close automatically and the liquid stays inside of the body.

Ryan quickly gets up and, with the heart in his hands, carefully walks over to the room where Ami is. He lays the heart he is holding in a square metal bin that is standing on one of the tables, and then focuses his attention on Ami.

He carefully walks over to her and, with all the care in the world, takes off her dress. With his heart pounding in his chest, he opens Ami's chest plate. The chest plate opens differently to the other AI, but Ryan can see that it is all the same basic concept. He very carefully unplugs Ami's heart; he can see the bullet hole that went straight through her, and he feels a pang in his own chest.

He lifts the heart from her chest and lays it onto

the table next to him. He then walks over to the metal bin and removes the heart. He walks back to Ami and very carefully places the heart in her chest and connects all the wires. He watches as the liquid fills the heart.

And then he waits.

Thirty seconds pass but still nothing happens.

Ryan leans over Ami and says to himself, 'Please. Please don't leave me.'

He starts to cry again, and a large tear rolls off his cheek and falls down on to Ami's heart, and suddenly a little shock of electricity sparks when it comes into contact with the heart.

Ryan is still crying, but then he notices that the heart is starting to light up. He takes a step back and sees that the heart is slowly starting to knock again. It beats faster and faster, and slowly it starts to glow brighter.

And then Ami opens her eyes and looks at Ryan. Ryan is crying and laughing with joy.

Ami lays her hand against Ryan's cheek and smiles up at him.

'Welcome back,' says Ryan.

ACKNOWLEDGEMENTS

Without question, Project Ami would not have been possible without my family and friends, and everyone else surrounding me, all of whom have supported me and helped me to get where I am at this very moment.

I also want to give special thanks to my parents, who not only have supported me tremendously throughout the course of my life, but also have been pivotal in allowing me to believe I can reach my goals.

And to my readers, I hope you have enjoyed the tale of Ryan and Ami. Writing this book has been an amazing experience, and so I very much look forward to penning further stories in the future.

CPSIA information can be obtained at www.ICGtesting.com
Printed in the USA
BVOW03s1405070416

443382BV00003B/11/P